Favored

A NOVEL

Sept 2 2022
Expressly for Gail
w/ Love!

Priscilla B Shuler
Priscilla B. Shuler

Copyright 2018 by Priscilla B. Shuler. All rights reserved.

Cover art by the author.
Layout by Rachel Newhouse for elfinpen designs.

This novel is dedicated to law enforcement personnel, everywhere... especially those who serve in the great state of South Carolina; and to one gentleman, in particular... James Arthur Turner, retired.

For His anger endureth but a moment;
in His favor is life:
weeping may endure for a night,
but joy cometh in the morning.

Psalm 30:5

CHAPTER 1

The Crime

The pounding on the soft, damp earth reverberated into her brain. Her first awareness came as an excruciating stab of pain in the back of her head. She screamed, but no sound was made nor heard.

Her eyelids were stuck closed. With a muddy hand she swiped across them, but realized she was probably making matters worse. She could feel the grit on her face. She struggled to get the hand free from her face. Numbness in her upper limbs made the attempt nigh on to impossible. With a burning determination she was able to move enough to begin to feel for the hem of her blouse and was horrified to find she had somehow lost it. *What happened to my blouse?* Weeping, she then gingerly forced her fingers on downward to feel for the white handkerchief she kept in the pocket of her blue jeans… which were also not on her body.

Loosening her struggle, she became aware that her eyes were opening, having been wet by her tears. Becoming ever more aware of her plight, she felt as if she'd been torn asunder. Attempting to recall her last thoughts, she was horrified to find she could not remember anything of where she had been, or now was.

What was the last thing she remembered? What was her name? Where was she? Why was she so cold, and naked? Was she blind? Deaf? Dead? No! No way could she be dead. She had known about always carrying a white handkerchief in her jeans. *Dead people surely would not think of such things.*

Suddenly she looked up and saw one glistening drop of water as it came toward her upturned face. She smiled as it struck her on her nose. Licking out her tongue, she tasted salty tears, snot and blood. She continued to weep gently, silently.

She attempted to rise, but collapsed in a heap. It was at that time she understood she'd been kept fairly warm beneath a heavy covering of leaves. *I'd better try to get up and out of here to see if I can find any way out of this place. Maybe I can see some lights somewhere. But, I don't want to be found with nothing on! Maybe I can wrap moss around myself, so I won't be so naked.*

Crawling in blinding pain, she felt for the nearest tree, and began to pull herself up. At that time, she felt herself being laid gently back down into the cocoon of leaves. She then realized that she'd never left the nest, but had simply been dreaming. Now, completely unable to move or moan she watched as the wavering lights and pounding feet rushed toward her. She knew she'd soon be all right. *I hate they're going to see me naked like this…….*

*

LeeRoy had come upon the gruesome scene around midnight. Finding her dead, he quickly left but stobbed forked limbs into the earth every few feet which could easily be seen by flashlight and headed home to get his truck and drive to the central area from where all the searchers had been dispatched. LeeRoy himself had never bothered to join with the other searchers. He had simply gone off on his own… following his intuition. Upon his return to the hastily established headquarters outside of the town proper, LeeRoy had no difficulty locating the Sheriff. Telling Boyd exactly where he could find her body, he then returned to his little cabin in the deep woods to mourn.

*

"Here! Junior! Get that light over here. I can see her hair even in this dark! Quick, hurry!"

As they played the light upon her form, Boyd screamed for the blanket.

Colleen was so relieved that she kept her eyes closed and tried to smile. Feeling herself covered in the blanket, she spoke her "Thank you…" but was unable to hear her words. She promptly returned to the safety of unconsciousness.

*

Opening her eyes, she found herself in a brilliant enclosure. There seemed to be light everywhere. Attempting to lift her right arm was unsuccessful. She glanced down and saw that her right arm was swathed in gauze and there were spots of blood that had seeped through. Glancing toward her left arm, she realized it was cast from elbow to fingertips. *My God, what have I done? How did this happen? What in the world have I been doing?* She shut her eyes and began to weep... tears flowing down her cheeks. Too, she knew her nose was dripping. *Oh, God. I cannot cry. I cannot even wipe my nose!* "Somebody! Somebody come help me, please!" This time she actually heard her voice, weak though it was.

Rustling through the open door, Nurse Blanch hurried to her bedside. "Oh, good! You're awake. We are all praying for you, sweetheart."

The nurse was adjusting something that was dripping into a clear tube. *She called me Sweetheart... She must know me.* Trying her voice once more, Colleen, asked, "What did I do? What has happened to me? Where am I?"

"There, there," answered Blanch with a soft pat upon Colleen's right leg. "You were found last night and brought into the emergency room." She turned and hummed softly as she adjusted the pillows and plumped the blankets around her torso. "You're gonna be just fine, Honey. The Doctors did a really good job of getting you all back together. It's just gonna take a little time is all."

She left the bedside and headed toward the door.

"Wait!" cried Colleen. "Talk to me a minute. Tell me everything you know about what happened to me. Did I have an awful accident? Was anyone else with me?" She was crying silently as huge tears rolled down her cheeks and soaked into the bandages wrapped around her head and down around her chin. "Why is my head hurting so? Please, don't leave. Help me understand. I cannot even recall who I am!" And she shook with constrained sobs. "Oh, I hurt so bad inside."

"Still in pain? I'll pump up the juice a little more. Maybe that'll help some."

Locating the proper meds, Blanch filled the hypo with an amount of morphine which she promptly fed into the clear tube running down into her right hand. "Now, you just relax. I must get back to the station. There are lots of other folks needing attention, so I want you to slip back into a nice sleep, so your body can heal. Doctor Hatfield will be in before long to check on you. You be sure and ask him all your questions. Okay?"

"Okay."

*

When Colleen opened her eyes this time, the room was much in shadow. Evidently the sun had slipped past its apex and was heading toward its bed. She could not see a clock, but surmised the hour to be around five in the afternoon. She knew they were in the throes of winter. She remembered taking down some Christmas decorations from someplace that was warm and cozy and smelled of French fries. Maybe that was her home? No, she didn't think so. Too many people there. Lots of tables and chairs. Her minds' eye led her through a swinging door into the heat of a busy kitchen. There was a friend working at assembling plates of foods, and a lady up to her elbows in salad greens. It was a comfort to her soul to feel the love within that space. *Where is this? Who are they? They're smiling at me, so they must know me.* She began weeping again.

"Don't cry, dear girl. You're going to be all right before long." Doctor Hatfield leaned over the injured girl, and 'shushed' her as he listened to her heart, and moved the stethoscope around her chest. He stood up and walked out.

Colleen heard him calling down the hall as he strode off to somewhere.

Within a few minutes she found herself surrounded with nurses, aides, and paraphernalia. They raised the head of the bed up-inch by inch, until they were satisfied. Her insides rebelled, but she kept silent since the pain and discomfort were easily bearable. She soon found herself beneath a clear tent with a slight hissing sound above her head.

Some nurse she'd not seen before patted her leg and told her to try to rest. "You're in good hands here. We'll see you through this, Colleen. Now, you relax and doze. I'll be back regularly to check in on you. If you become distressed, press this little red button here." And she held up a small white cord to which was attached a white cylinder with the red button at the end. "Are you right handed, or left?"

"Right, I guess."

"Of course. You couldn't hold this thing in your left hand, now could you?" And she tittered. "Here then, you hold this in your right hand. I feel sure you can move your thumb down strong enough to press it." She snugged the control into Colleen's hand and said, "Push it."

It took a few seconds before they were rewarded with the entrance of yet another nurse Colleen had never seen. They both smiled and assured her that she was their top priority.

"We're right down the hall. All you have to do is push the button if you need anything, and someone will be right in. Now, don't you worry. All right?"

"Wait, please. Tell me why the Doctor had y'all put this plastic over my bed? What's it for?"

Smiling, the lovely young woman said, "Doctor Bradley was a little concerned when he found a small amount of fluid in your lungs. He wanted to make sure you were raised up some and could get plenty of air to help you breathe easier. It'll be taken away soon. Don't you worry."

"Thank you." She settled back onto the raised bed and opened her mind to her situation. *So! My name is Colleen. Colleen What? Maybe it'll come back to me soon, and I might recall what awful accident I had.* She breathed deeply, nodded, and laid the control down by her side and drifted back into the arms of Morpheus.

Sheriff was even acquainted with the man to any extent. And, could have cared less anyway. This man gave Boyd an edge no one else was aware of.

*

The place where Colleen had been found had already been cordoned off by Boyd's people and the local loner-a 50 something Vietnam vet who preferred the wild animals to any man, anytime- had been posted nearby to guard the place. As Horace and Frederick stood at the perimeter of the area, outside the scene proper, Horace spoke, "Do you suppose these yokels have destroyed any possibility we might have in finding anything of value to the case over yonder?" He nodded toward the mound of leaves that had covered the body.

"Ain't no 'yokels' around these parts but you two idiots! You couldn't find your asses with a cow prod and a lightnin' bolt!"

The pair of newcomers jumped as if they'd been stabbed with a hot poker! "What 'th hell!?!" They turned in tandem and glared at the camouflaged man. "Who the hell are you and what in the hell do you think you're doing?"

The man stuck out a dirty hand and spat a stream of tobacco juice about four feet across the leaves. "My name is Roy-short for LeeRoy. An' I'm set here by my Sheriff to see to it that nobody innerferes with this here crime scene. I can tell right off that you two don't know squat about solving nothin'! Why you two dunderheads walked right in front of my tent back yonder and with me a-settin in front of th' damn thang!"

Both men turned to look back toward the direction from which they'd come, and sure enough, there was a small tent, albeit, camouflaged. Turning back to LeeRoy, they realized they were in foreign territory and needed to reconnoiter their positions. Fred reached out and took the dirty proffered hand

and shook it firmly, "Sorry about that, SIR. We're just like everybody else… speaking when we ought to be listening, I guess." Letting go of the hand, and suppressing the surging desire to wipe it on something, he continued, "My name is Fred, and my Assistant is Horace Godbold."

"Assistant, my ass! Where do you get such brass? You're the assistant and I'm lead man."

"Who did you get that from? I distinctly remember, when we were brought in that George called my name first, so that makes you my assistant. And besides, you do know 'F' comes before 'H', don't you?"

"Shit! That just shows how much you know! It's last names that count! And 'G' is before "SHIT" in any man's dictionary!"

"Fellas! Fellas! Enough! Lets just us try to git along now and get some work done. We all want to solve the mystery of who tried to kill the 'Sweetheart of THE 95'. So, here." Lifting the yellow tape, he invited the pair to enter cautiously-which they did.

LeeRoy stood immobile outside the perimeter as he watched the men work from opposite sides toward each other. Picking up miniscule items which they placed in Ziploc bags. He listened as they spoke in whispers, but LeeRoy heard every word. His hunter's ears were fine-tuned to hear nearly as good as any wild animal he tracked in these very woods.

He knew they'd found some piece of small jewelry, a shred of torn fabric that could have been from her cotton blouse… still had a button attached. The perpetrator evidently had carried off her clothing and shoes as no other pieces of apparel were found. They did find plenty of her hair. She'd been beset upon somewhere else and brought into these woods. Here, she'd been beaten to a pulp, raped and left for dead. They determined the devil had then kicked leaves upon her body in a quick attempt to cover his murderous rampage.

Coming back to the yellow tape where LeeRoy had it lifted for them, Horace had an idea to get some free help. "Man, would you help us by using your hunting abilities?"

Straightening up somewhat, LeeRoy answered, "Sure. I'd love to be of help in gettin' this son'a'bitch what done this to our girl."

"Good! Just what I wanted to hear. I need you to answer my questions for me to know you have the expertise in what we're gonna want from you. "

"Sure. Shoot."

"How long you been hunting?"

"Since I was seven or eight, I guess. I know all the woods around here like the back of my hand."

"Wonderful! Now, can you search a place and not mess up anything that could be evidence?"

"Why, of course! Any good woodsman can do that. Never want to mess up tracks or the scent."

"Scent?"

"Yeah. Scent! Scent is what you follow and what follows you. Any hunter worth his salt has to get rid of his own scent so the animal won't know when you're on his tail."

"Here! Let me shake your hand again! You're our man of the hour! You're going to help us solve this case. With your brawn and our brains, we're going to have this murdering sonofabitch before we can say 'howdydoo'."

"Boy, oh boy. I'm happy to help. But you gotta tell me what it is that I'm to be a'trackin'."

Lifting the yellow tape, Horace took LeeRoy over to the pile of leaves. Pointed to where they could see the swipes of a boot where it had swept the leaves up and over the body. The men both showed him how to read the motions of struggle, the attempts to run, the dragging, the bludgeoning, the blood- soaked earth, knee holes formed by the actual raping. When the three stood again LeeRoy was crying in sobs. "By God, boys, I'll get this spawn of Satan for you. You don't worry about that." Wiping his nose with his sleeve, he continued, "I'll need to get permission from the Sheriff to leave off guarding this place, though."

"Oh naw, LeeRoy, don't you worry about that. We'll talk to the Sheriff for you as soon as we get back to town. But you stay on your post for now, 'cause you never know if the would-be murderer might just come back to the scene of his crime. We'll be back in touch with you before this day gets dark. And don't tell a living soul what you're going to do to help in this. You don't want to be alerting anybody! Mum's the word, Man."

"Mum's the word? Sure! Mum's the word."

LeeRoy shook his head slowly as he watched the pair stumble back to where they'd parked. He grinned and spat another steaming streak of juice against the base of a large pin oak. *Them little city boys have no inkling of exactly who they were messin' with.* Grinning, he turned and shimmied up the oak until he was high enough to watch them picking their dainty shoes back toward their car. Reaching out he swept his dirty hand over the back of a drowsy fox squirrel...

His eyes never left the pair. They stepped carefully leaving the area and heading back to where Deputy Raeford had led them to park their vehicle… to exactly the path formed that lead to the crime scene. The little-used dirt road could only be called a road because it forked off from the country road which wound itself behind the long, tall fencing of the Harrison Hotel Complex-through the white-washed shacks nestled by the open cotton fields. Why, the nameless road was only drivable simply because the hunters kept the ruts open with their trucks. The dead, weedy center growing between the ruts, swept the underbelly of any vehicle attempting to travel it. Even the tall-wheeled monster trucks everyone hated parking next to at the Walmart parking lot weren't exempt.

CHAPTER 3

The Ruse

"Yeah… if'n it hadn't a been for LeeRoy Hasgrove, our girl might'n never have been found." Declared Colonel.

"I agree! He hunts all over this county."

The company all laughed. Cletus said, "Yeah, in season or out. Makes no difference to him!" Then he spoke quiet-like. "You know what? I'll betch'all all I own that he'll find out who done this too."

"You reckon?" Asked Jolene.

"Sure's I'm cookin' hash today!" And the company laughed.

"Then it's a sure thing, ain't it?"

They all nodded and stirred their coffee and glanced around at each other.

"It's back in the kitchen for me, then." Said Cletus. But before he could get turned around, Colonel caught his attention.

"If they really wanted to catch that devil then they'd declare our Colleen to've passed on, and they'd hold a funeral and all. Nobody but those needing to know would know she's still strugglin' on."

"You mean by everybody thinkin' she's dead and gone, the killer will get careless and show hisself?"

"Something like that. Maybe."

"Aw, Colonel. Ain't no way anything like that gonna be kept a secret. We'd all be wanting to still check up on her ever day. No Sir! No way could all of us keep such a secret," declared Margie.

"That's because you ain't got the desire, Margie. Any secret can be kept if the outcome is important enough."

"I suppose so. But I'd do just about anything to help get whoever dun this to our Colleen."

Chester (Colonel) Jones looked around at the sparcely inhabited dining room. There was just himself, Margie, Milford, Selma, Jolene and Cletus. He spoke up and said, "How many of y'all think you … No! How many of y'all KNOW you can keep such an important secret?"

"You mean about Colleen a'dyin?" asked Margie.

"Yes! That's what we've been talkin' about all this time, now ain't it?" Colonel was getting a little overheated, and no one wanted to witness one of his 'meltdowns'.

"All right, all right. Let's raise our hands. Those of us committed to keeping such an important secret."

Five pair of hands went up. Margie looked at Colonel, and asked, "Well, what about you?"

"My God, Margie! Of course, I will. After all, I'm the one what thought of it, now ain't I?" He put his hand up and then lowered it as the rest of the company did likewise. "Now! Y'all are to forget all about this little pact we've made. Don't tell anybody, and I do mean anybody. I've gotta go talk to the Sheriff to see if he's on board with this ploy. If he ain't, then the whole thing is a 'no go'. Understand?"

They all nodded.

Colonel slid off the stool and left a dollar on the counter.

"You don't need to leave no money. You know your coffee is always on the house," said Selma.

Chester paused at the door, turned and grinned, and said, "I know, but I hit the jackpot early this morning from a car headed to Fayetteville. They were taking their boy up to Camp LeJeune, and they saw I was a vet. I think everybody in that car emptied their pockets for me. They gave me enough for a month's supply of grub." And he left quickly and headed off toward town to visit with Sheriff Boyd.

*

It just so happened that the suggestion brought by Colonel was what one could term, 'a day late and a dollar short'. Boyd had already begun the ball to rolling to cover the 'death' of Colleen, but he certainly did not share that vital information with Colonel. Sheriff Boyd already had wheels set in motion, that no one, but he and Doctor Hatfield were privy to.

"I sincerely appreciate the fine suggestion you brought, but I'm afraid our Colleen is already on the brink. They are doing all they can for her, but if she makes it, it'll be by some miracle." Said Boyd. "But keep this bit of information under your belt. Don't relate it to anyone. Just tell your folks out at THE 95 that you couldn't find me today. Okay?" He clapped his hand on the shoulder of Chester, before turning back toward his desk-piled high with papers.

Suddenly looking back up toward his guest, he continued, "But I want to let you know how much we appreciate you and THE 95 crew for coming up with this ploy, but most of all for wanting to help us. It's folks like y'all that make our job worthwhile and keeps us on our toes."

As soon as Colonel was out of the building, Boyd turned and hollered to Nancy, "Git th' Coroner on the phone!"

*

Coroner Talbert Lamar came on board with Boyd's ploy concerning the 'death' of Colleen. He sent a message FYEO to the County Attorney, Amanda Harris, giving her a heads-up as to the death of the victim. A Doctor Bradley had already been contacted by Doctor Hatfield, and soon showed up with his assistant to accept the care of Colleen. No one at Zacchary General had ever seen him before but did not question his appearance. His orders were met with no resistance, since Doctor Hatfield himself had been adamant about their appreciation of his involvement and expertise with the patient. His every word was to be considered law!

About a week after the arrival of Doctor Bradley, in the dead of night, a black hearse silently waited out in a side lot-away from the emergency entrance. A gurney was wheeled out of a seldom-used exit door and quickly lifted into the vehicle. The few who happened to be on duty that night, were never aware of the activity.

Upstairs in the room where Colleen had been sequestered, two recently hired cleaning women, under the direction of Doctor Hatfield, were sorting out the few flowers and gifts that had been left for her. They were careful to leave the bed and equipment as though the patient had just gone to the bathroom and would return soon.

Next morning at the seven o'clock shift change, the on-comers were shocked to find their star patient had suddenly died just an hour before. Everyone rushed to the room and from there down to the morgue. Rushing back to the second floor, screaming, "What have y'all done with her?" demanded Christine Blanchard!

"Why, she's been transported to Columbia for autopsy, Christine," answered Doctor Hatfield, with gentle words.

"Oh, my God! And I thought she was beginning to rally. I swear she said she was having lots less pain. Why, she was even moving the fingers on her left hand too. We even had her sitting up on the bedpan!" She wailed. "I simply cannot accept this! Have you told Doctor Bradley?"

"Calm down, Christine. I realize this is a shock, but if you peruse her chart you might understand the onset of MERSA. Doctor Bradley was here until about an hour ago, when she succumbed. Of course. He was called in last night when she became critical. Her fever spiked, and we were unable to halt the upward swing. Even packed in ice, she could not regain a hold on recovery. I'm truly sorry. She was a lovely young woman, and you know we all shall miss her."

He turned to go, and then said, "I'll go ahead and call the Zacchary Times. They'll be wanting to come get the full story, I'm sure."

*

Jerry Arnold, with his steno pad and pencil stub, along with his daughter, Bess, a budding photographer, arrived at the hospital by 8:15. Stopping at the small information window, he showed his 'press' card and asked where the room of Colleen Woodard had been. "I need to get some pictures, please. If I may."

"Of course. Second floor, room 205-right two doors after you leave the stairwell."

Bounding the steps two at a time, they arrived to watch and record the scene of the bed being stripped, the oxygen tent being disassembled, the rubber ice mattress being emptied, the wheeled IV stand which held half empty bags of some fluid or other being rolled out the door and down the hall. Before five minutes had passed, Jerry wrote his thoughts and Bess had taken a number of poignant shots of the empty, pristine room in which had lain the suffering body of Colleen Woodard. How tragic.

When the photos were shown on TV that night, everyone in the county was devastated! They had begun following the news of this beautiful young woman. She had become everyone's best friend, or at least they could recall the time they'd stopped to chat and pass time with her at THE 95 Truck Stop. Deepest struck were the regulars. Truck drivers who frequented the place simply because they came to love being in her presence. They'd ply her with small gifts and remembrances from places they'd been in their big rigs. Each one enamored more with every time they were in her presence. But even they knew she was unattainable. Colleen never gave anyone the idea that she had a favorite. The only name she ever put forth as truly meaning anything to her was that of her child, Eddie. She kept a crumpled snapshot of him in the pocket of any uniform she wore. It had been cut away from a picture someone had taken of him with his father. She'd cut off the section of husband, Bobby Woodard, and burned it in the flame of her apartment-size gas range.

*

The issue containing the obituary of the 'Sweetheart of THE 95 Truck Stop', appeared on the second page of the local newspaper. Editor Willie Wilcox wanted to do her proud, and so surrounded the item with gray printed strands of ivy. Everyone that saw it told him it was a real fitting tribute to 'their girl'.

Colleen Rebecca Spires Woodard, 29, of 673 Thrift Court, a long-time resident of Zacchary was born September 17, 1970 to the late Wilma Pinallo Spires and the late Lester Henry Spires. Colleen is also predeceased by an older brother, Lester Spires, Jr. She is survived by her ex-husband, Robert Edwin Woodard and a son, Albert 'Eddie' Edwin Woodard, aged 9, of unknown whereabouts. Funeral arrangements to be handled by Willingham's, with interment in the Oakmont Cemetery on highway six. The memorial service will be graveside, weather permitting, at three o'clock Saturday January 23, 1999.

CHAPTER 4

Slow Recovery

Betty adjusted the blue blanket again, over the legs of Colleen. "Honey, you just let me know if I can help you to the john. You haven't been since you woke up. Don't you need to go yet?"

"I don't feel like I do. But, maybe I need to see. I probably will once I get set down. Here, help me."

Betty threw the blanket aside and helped to swing her legs over the edge, and steadied her to stand. They moved in tandem, Betty rolling the IV stand behind them, into the toilet. Since she was still very unsteady on her feet, Betty had to aid in the sitting, cleaning, and standing again. Success. They toiled together back to the bed where she again made her charge comfortable.

"Tell me about yourself, please," spoke Colleen, "and why you're here with me, and how long I've been here? And where is this place?"

Betty nodded and smiled. "I imagine you do need some questions answered." She made herself comfortable and sat close to the bedside. "You were brought to this facility last week. Your Doctor felt you needed constant 'round the clock attention and your home hospital simply wasn't equipped with the staff to handle such a need. Consequently, he contacted us to bring you here and care for you." She continued, "Are you aware that you did not have an accident?"

"I'd kinda' come to that conclusion. With a broken left hand and arm, and the bruising and tenderness of my right one, as well as my head having been broken open, I couldn't figure how in the world I'd done something to cause this. I cannot recall anything about it. And just in the past several hours I've begun to have awful pictures come into my head of some man really mad with me." She began to weep gently, "And, I wonder how my body got so sore and bruised. Even my legs have stitches where I've been cut open." Lifting her reddened, tear stained face to Betty, "What in the world happened to me? I want to know."

Betty sat forward and placed the small recorder on the dinner tray, and asked Colleen to repeat what she just said.

"Okay. I can see snatches of myself being dragged and slapped and pulled out of a car, or maybe it's a truck. Anyway, it's very dark and cold. I can hear the river or some stream or other." She stopped and shook her head gently. "Oh, that still hurts when I shake my head. What did he do to me?"

Betty snapped off the recorder.

"Well, you know Doctor Hatfield planned all this out." She waved her hand around to indicate the room they were in. "All for your safety and to possibly aid in the finding of the person that hurt you." She stopped, then decided to continue. "You do know, now don't you, that someone tried to kill you. In fact, whoever it was is now certain that they succeeded. The word is out that you died in the hospital down in Zacchary. Up here nobody knows who you are except that you're a special patient of Doctor Bradley's. They've registered you under a different name too."

"Really? Why, what is my name now?" She laughed a little, and said, "I just now learned what my real name is and now I've been given another one?"

"Yes. It's because they don't want anyone to guess that you're alive. You see, they're working like crazy to try to figure out who hurt you, so they can charge him. That is if they ever find him."

"So, what's my name?"

"You are now known as Jane Dooley. I guess that's as close as they could come to the proverbial 'Jane Doe'. So, try to remember who you are when someone comes in to see Jane." She sat beside the bed in a recliner chair and continued to talk. "For your information, my name really is Betty. It's Betty Copeland. Doctor Bradley is my uncle and I've worked with him for years. He sent me through nursing school and after I graduated, he hired me for his special cases. He works all over the United States on cases where his expertise is needed… such as you. I will be your constant companion until such time as you can return to your life or be given a new identity for your protection. Whoever is out there is thinking you're dead. If you are to reenter society without him being found, then your looks must be altered, and a new identity provided. You won't ever be able to return to the life you once had. It'd be too dangerous. If he suspects you're alive to identify him, then he'll do all in his power to kill you again."

"But, I can't tell anyone who he is. I cannot remember anything about any of the attack."

"Yeah, but he doesn't know that. He would never give you the opportunity to finger him if he knew you were alive. That's why all this secrecy and underhandedness is going on. We need to protect you on every hand. And, dear... if by a miracle your memory returns, then you must tell me every detail you can recall. I'll record your every word. Okay?"

"Sure. I just hope I can remember more, even though I'm really scared about it. I cannot figure why anyone would want to kill me in the first place."

"Truth be told, I don't think he set out to kill you in the beginning. I think you fought like a tiger and he broke you up so badly before the rape until he figured he'd better go ahead and get you out of your misery, so you could never tell anyone who he is, or describe him, either."

"Oh, no. You mean I was raped too? Oh, God. Who would do such a thing?" She laid back and looked at the ceiling. "I guess I'm just grateful to still be alive... and I want to get to see my son again one of these days." She looked over at Betty. "I've been saving money, so I could hire somebody to try to find him."

"Wonderful! So, you've now remembered you have a child. How old is your boy now?"

"Yes! I had no idea my memory would begin to return like this." She smiled, then continued, "Yes, and I believe they might be out west somewhere. Bobby, the man I was married to, was always saying how he'd love to live in Wyoming or Utah. I just know that's probably where they ended up." She began to weep again... "My son is nine now. Bobby took him from the school that I'd just enrolled him in. They said that Bobby came and picked him up right after they let out and they rode off in Bobby's rig. He was never seen again. The dispatcher had no idea where he'd gone after he offloaded that last time. He wouldn't respond or anything. He must'a had it planned for a while. But it sure devastated me. I didn't have an inkling that Bobby wasn't happy with our marriage, or that he'd ever steal my baby! He'd barely turned six when it happened."

Betty felt useless as she watched the floodgates open. "I know it's hard on you, honey, but God is a just God and you'll be rewarded one of these days. Just be patient and keep praying."

"That's all I can do, and then when I get well maybe I can find somebody who can find him once all this is cleared up." She looked out the window at the gray skies and lightly falling snow. "Has Doctor Bradley said anything at all about when I would be able to feed myself or get this gauze off my head? Did they shave my head, Betty?"

"I don't think they shaved all of it. Just the top and back where they had to do some surgery. And I think they probably cut the rest of it short to make keeping it clean easier."

"I'll be glad to see my whole head again. Do you think he'll be in to change the bandages today?"

"Oh, yes. He'll be in before the afternoon is half gone. Surely before time for your dinner meal-such as it is." She smiled, looking up at the clear fluid rolling down the tube. "You'll be ready for a more substantial food before you know it."

"Good. I wish we had some of Cletus's Barbeque. He makes the best in the world. It's famous all the way up and down I-95. Which reminds me. I can remember just about everything about THE 95 Truck Stop and a lot of the regulars who come there. If you get the recorder, I feel like talking some while I've got the chance."

"Great!" She clicked the little recorder back on. "You go ahead and talk away, honey."

CHAPTER 5

Getting Down to Business

Sunday night, January 24, Sheriff Boyd Custer drove out to LeeRoy's place. It was after nine o'clock and Boyd knew he'd be already in bed. The dirt road was dark as the inside of a cow, but he drove slow, and sensed his way. The deep ruts more or less kept the car between the ditches. He just gave the wheel very little in the way of help and rolled silently onward until he could make out the old dilapidated fence gate. His eyes had adjusted very well to the minimal light of the quarter moon shining through the leafless trees. As soon as he spied the house, he cut the engine and walked toward it. He began to 'owl hoot' and click to mimic the sound of a coon. By the time he reached the porch, LeeRoy invited him inside.

Once seated at the small table-still in the cloying dark, Boyd said, "I'm gonna be needin' your help, Bro. I need to know I can count on you with this mission."

"Sheriff, you know you can. I'll do everthing I can to help out. I guess you already know them two city slickers've enlisted my help to do some trackin' for 'em." He smiled in the dark. Boyd could just barely make out his white teeth, and wondered how his friend was able to keep them so white what with all the tobacco chewing he did. He'd never seen Roy without a wad in his cheek.

"I figured they'd need help from some quarter. What'd you tell 'em?"

"I told 'em exactly what I just told you."

"You been out working yet?"

"Yep. I did a little look-see just at daybreak this morning. You know, when the dew is fresh, and the bruised grasses show where any activity has occurred."

"You gotta know you're the world's best tracker, LeeRoy Hasgrove. I've seen you do the impossible. In fact, those two State boys were sure as hell bent all outa shape about how you snuckered 'em that day at the crime scene." He snickered gently, and continued. "They never said anything to any of us about it, but they were overheard out at THE 95 whispering about you and your invisibility! Boy, you had 'em really shook!" Boyd paused, then he went on. "Now, what I'm wanting you to do is go around wherever you are going around as sneaky as possible. I want you to listen when nobody knows you're anywhere near. Keep everything you happen to hear as near to exact as you can. I'll come out here every night like this and you can tell me what you know. If you don't know anything new, don't worry about it, but just keep on keepin' on with trying." He stopped, looked through the dark into LeeRoy's face, "But, the most important thing I need you to do is daytime reconnaissance, without making any sign you've been anywhere in the area I want you to go."

"Where is that, Sheriff?"

"I want you to go to the place where we found her body, and I need you to work backward to figure out how she got there. See if you can picture how big or small the man was that murdered her. See how she struggled. Where he brought her into the woods from. Just work your way back to see if you can come up with how he brought her to the place." He sat silent for a moment, listening to LeeRoy breathe. "Then maybe you can tell where he headed out to next. He had to've dumped the clothes somewhere. We've searched everywhere we can think of to see if we could find them. Think you can help me with this?"

"All I can say is, I'll do everything God gives me the power to do to get as much information back to you as I can." He stood up. "But you might's as well wait for two or three days… I mean nights, before you come back out here. I might not be here all the time for a few nights. I believe I can listen out to a lot of conversations outside of the dives around here. Maybe I can come up with something. Okay?"

Boyd stood, and reached out in the dark to shake the hand of his best and most secret weapon in his fight against crime in Zacchary. He'd put LeeRoy on the payroll if it were possible, but that would alert everyone to exactly who was the crime solver and ruin his reputation as being the best in South Carolina!

*

That evening out at THE 95 Truck Stop the entire crew looked as if they'd witnessed some horrible event. And indeed, they had. "D'ya suppose we caused her to go and die?" Asked Margie.

"No! Why would you even come up with such of a thing? We can't cause a body to die just by thinkin' it."

"Well, you know… maybe the power of suggestion, or something…"

"Don't be stupid. Colleen had no idea that we came up with the idea of her dyin'. And, even if she did, I know good and well she wouldn't do it on purpose."

"Yes. Doc says she contracted some kinda bad bacteria and it just flooded her system. She couldn't fight it off."

All heads were cast down and tears flowed easily. About that time the door jingled open and Junior came in with a blast of cold air. "What's everbody lookin' so gloomy for? Y'all act like it's th' end of th' world, or somethin'."

"Oh, Junior. You ain't got a sympathetic bone in your body! We're all in here mourning our loss and you come blastin' in like some hoity toity know-it-all! Ain't you got no manners?"

"Well, 'scuse me for livin'! I'm truly sorry the girl died, but it ain't the end of the world, y'all know. There'll be somebody else to come along what'll take her place here. But I'm sorry y'all, I really didn't mean to sound so careless about her, but life does go on, you know." *You fools got no idea how much I miss her either,* he thought. *I just can't let my feelings show!*

Cletus came around the counter and grabbed his collar and shoved him out the door. "Yeah, Well, we're sorry too, but we don't want your ugly face around here right now either." He slammed it and locked it. Stood and watched as Junior pounded on the glass and cussed them all to hell. Spittle spattering down his chin in droplets.

Turning back toward the group inside THE 95 Restaurant, Cletus asked, "How about another cup, y'all? It's almost closing time for this shift, and we might as well finish it off before I get another pot a'goin'."

Holding his cup up, Colonel said, "I'll have another, then I must be leaving for my humble abode."

As Margie filled the cup, she asked, "You got enough warm covers out there? It's supposed to be pretty cold tonight. Down in the low fortys I think."

"Indeed, I do. Bought a new flannel lined jump suit from Curtis just last week. Y'all know he always roams the secondhand places for me and he found it for a couple of dollars. It has a hole or two… like where a mouse might'a been chewing, but that don't hurt it a bit. When I crawl into that thing, and keep my wool socks on, why I'm warm as toast."

"I'm glad for you, Colonel." She smiled at him.

The group was silent for a few seconds, then they all turned at the loud pounding at the front door. Everyone laughed as Cletus ran to unlock it. An irate trucker swept inside. "Why th' hell you got the damn door locked? I thought you were open all night."

"Sorry about that, friend. We are open." He laughed. "I just forgot. Had to get rid of a 'Rowdy' a little while back and forgot to unlock it after he was gone." He patted the burly man on his shoulder, and said, "Now you just come on in and find a place. We'll have you taken care of before you can count to ten!"

*

Sheriff Boyd called on Mister Willingham on Jan 26 to discuss the idea of holding a memorial service for the deceased victim. The state would reimburse any expenses incurred by those needing to participate in this service. Boyd knew the town needed some closure to the loss of one so well loved by the common people of the surrounding area. Colleen-he had to admit, was truly 'one in a million' type of person. She would be missed by everyone who ever knew her, and many would miss her simply because she'd become such an undeserving victim.

Todd Willingham, owner of Willingham's Funeral Home seemed delighted to provide everything in the way of casket, flowers, and bulletins, as well as getting the Fowlard Brothers to dig the site out at Oakmont. At least, that was the impression he had given Sheriff Custer. Of course, he knew the casket would be empty, as the body would be cremated by the state after the autopsy, but it was all necessary for the town to have a funeral for closure to the life of such a beloved woman.

Todd could be considered the proverbial undertaker. He was tall, thin, bald, and silent. Wore nothing but black… Oh, his shirts were stiffly starched and white as white could be, but then all his ties were black bow ties. Shoes, black patent. His ever-handy handkerchiefs were woven of the finest linen but edged in a small band of black, with initials of *TW* embroidered in one corner. No one ever found themselves holding one of his handkerchiefs at any visitation or funeral but what they always returned said handkerchief laundered and pressed.

If he'd liked women, he supposed that Colleen might be at the top of a 'worthy' list. But, being as how he preferred young men, the idea of lamenting the demise of any woman simply brought no concern to him. He'd use his cheapest box and a small spray-enough to make the effort, and do his part for the townspeople, although he'd already figured an inflated bill to present for reimbursement.

*

Then there was Preacher David Abner, the Pastor to Colleen since he and his family had come to Zacchary from Lincolnton, Georgia back in 1986, was also agreeable to conduct the memorial service. "I'll do whatever God'll allow to help bring honor for the lady." He assured the Sheriff.

To David, she was without doubt the most stunning girl he'd ever seen. When he had taken the pulpit for his initial sermon, he could barely keep his eyes off the fatherless child. She'd been sixteen years old, with a soft, svelte figure, long white-blond hair, and mesmerizing blue eyes. Through the weeks, he began to lament that her dresses were all sewn of shapeless, waistless, buttonless cotton which her destitute mother made from the same pattern. Cutting subsequent dresses just a tad larger or longer as she grew. He took his concern to his wife.

Mary Abner found it an unexpected pleasure to gift the young girl with her old clothes. Some of which fit, and some which didn't… those were cut apart and used any way possible to reassemble into some of the most god-awful combinations known to modern man. But, Colleen wore everything her mother came up with and never said a word. Her classmates seldom had any verbal offering concerning her attire, except when she wore something that looked rather appealing. Then they over-compensated in their remarks, making Colleen determined to wear those particular dresses more than usual. Soon the ploy turned on her by the beloved dresses becoming worn out with washing, or coming apart at the seams, or shrinking because the item had needed to be dry cleaned, but had, instead been washed.

At least, she could not be found slacking in her attempt to help the child when the need had been so blatant. Truly, Mary 'saved' Colleen's teen years by literally dressing the girl singlehandedly. And Mary made sure all her husband's parishioners knew about her benevolence. Why, for her graduation from high school, Mary had brought a large box containing a half-dozen unmentionables, freshly laundered and still with the elastic in good shape. No one could fault her for not doing everything in her power to help the poor child.

CHAPTER 6

West Virginia

A cold fog lay over the valley. Bobby had stepped out onto the porch of his cabin. Old Sol was rising dead ahead and he was content with his world. Wrapped in a heavy blanket, his feet encased in thick woolen slippers, he sat and rocked as he sipped the steaming coffee. He could hear his woman messing around in the kitchen and the soft mumbling voice of his son. The bus wouldn't be by today, but his newspaper would. Up here he always got the paper a couple days late, but that was all right. He still was able to kinda connect with the home he'd left behind over three years before. *Here she comes now.* He stepped off the porch and down onto the pebbled path to greet Sarah Craig as she brought her Bronco to a skidding halt. Grinning, she handed the paper and a couple of ads out to Bobby and said, "You shore do look plum sexy wrapped all up in that blanket! Why I'll bet Ashe is a'layin' in bed wishing you'd git yore behind on back in there."

He guffawed. "Yeah. And I bet you left your man dead to the world when you took off this morning!"

"Oh Yeah. Melvin loves a warm bed on a cold morning."

"Don't we all. Have a good day and and keep 'er between th' ditches."

He swatted the rolled-up paper against her arm as she drove off down the mountain.

*

Slamming back into the cabin, he said, "Ashe, can you and Eddie take care of yourselves for a few days alone?"

"What's the matter, Bobby? You're white as a ghost! What's wrong?"

Drawing in a calming breath and looking over at his son slurping through a large bowl of Sweet Puffs and whole milk, he shook his head, and lowered his voice and motioned to Ashe. "Come into the bedroom a minute."

"Let me turn off the eye… I'll be right there."

*

"Honey, something awful has happened down home. Eddie's mama is dead. She was murdered…" Shaking his head, with tears shimmering in his eyes. "I can't believe it. Who on God's green earth would do such a thing. Honest to God, she was the most agreeable bitch I ever knew. Seemed as though everybody loved her… that is, except me. I just never got around to it, I guess." Pausing to gaze back toward the closed door to the room where Eddie was eating his breakfast, he said. "I want to go down for a few days. At least to go to the funeral. Will you and Eddie be okay?"

"Sure, Hon. Just get me to Piggly Wiggly so I can stock up and won't need to leave the cabin 'til you can get back."

"Good. Get dressed and we'll go this morning. I'd like to leave today, if possible. I'll call Glenn and tell him I won't be drivin' for a few days. He won't care when I tell him why."

*

Bobby kissed his wife and son goodbye and drove off in the only vehicle they owned… a gray Ford Focus. He just hoped it would hold up for the trip. He figured he'd be able to pull into Zacchary this time tomorrow. He could find a motel to set up camp in until he could get around to talking with the certain folks he felt might give him the time of day. Many of the friends he and Colleen had, had simply turned their backs on him after he left. He'd tried to contact them to see how she was faring, but not one soul would suffer him to speak to them about anything, let alone Colleen.

However, there was one person he knew was still very interested in him and the dead relationship between him and Colleen. That was Junior Raeford. Junior had always been available whenever he'd wanted to complain about Colleen. Junior verbally commiserated with the pitiful excuses of the man as he told of his unhappiness. They shared can after can of warm beer together. Bobby could be counted on to sway his best friend to begin a heavy dose of cussin' about women in general, and Colleen in particular. Junior was the only one who could salve his conscience and assure him that he had been terribly wronged by that bitch of a woman! Then, having his backbone stiffened by flattery, Bobby knew that he'd be met with silence and a cold shoulder once he decided to stagger home. Boy, Colleen sure knew how to emasculate a man.

Funny, now Ashe was totally different. Of course, he no longer drank, or screwed around like he had in the past.

*

Pulling into the Marvel Motel out at the 95-26 intersection, Bobby had no trouble obtaining a room… fairly clean and with an attached greasy spoon, it was exactly to his liking. He planned his day for tomorrow, Jan 29th. He'd seen that the funeral was set for 2:30 out at Oakmont, but that gave him plenty of time to try to make contact with Junior in the morning.

After a filling and satisfying supper of country ham, grits, scrambled eggs, and biscuits… washed down with three cups of coffee-liberally laced with sugar, he paid up, left a tip of two dollars, and walked the twenty yards back to his room.

Piling into bed, fully dressed except for his shoes, he dialed home. Ashe answered on the second ring. Bobby talked a couple minutes with her then asked to speak to Eddie. "I'm sorry, hon. He's in the shower. In fact, he just started, and you know how long he takes to finish. He's either the cleanest or the dirtiest boy in West Virginia." She laughed lightly.

"Well, okay. But you tell him I called and wanted to talk to him, now, hear?"

"Sure. You know I will." There was a loud silence, then she asked, "Did you make the trip okay? No car trouble?"

"Naw. But the deer were sure out all over the place. I was okay, but some unlucky bastard following me sure got him one though. I could see him screeching across the road. I lost sight. I hope he didn't go over the edge. Poor bastard."

"Oh, my God! Bobby. Didn't you stop to see about it? It could'a been a carload of people… a family with little children!"

"For heaven's sake, Ashe. There were cars on back. I feel sure some of them were better able to stop. I was already out of range and it would'a been dangerous if I'd'a slammed on brakes. Better for everyone for me to keep goin'. You're just lettin' your sympathy rule over your better judgement. That's exactly why women ought never be in combat."

"Oh Lord! We're on this kick again. Just because Brandy joined doesn't affect me one iota. Why, I'd rather be your wife and a stay-at-home step mom than crawling in some foxhole." Again, the loud silence. "Well, hon. Send me a goodnight kiss, and let me get up from here and clean up this kitchen."

"Goodnight, Ashe. I'll take better care of you when I get back home."

"Do you know how long you'll be down there?"

"Not more'n two or three days. I'll call you when I'm ready to head back out. Nite, hon."

"Okay. I better get off. Call me when you head back this way. Love you, Bobby. G'nite."

CHAPTER 7

The Memorial Service

It was downright cold that afternoon-January 29th. Todd estimated the attendance at around seventy-five souls. Of course, THE 95 Truck Stop was well represented, as well as most of those from the nearby areas that had known Colleen as she'd grown up there. Then, there were the curious who'd read of the murder and all its gory details in several issues of the local rag that covered and recovered everything that the reporters could glean as well as some nicely formed additions of the 'surely occurred' events.

Three eulogies were given by close friends-Selma-wife and co-owner of THE 95 read from a sheet of notebook paper, on which a number of THE 95ers had given input. Then Colonel had asked to be allowed to speak. He spoke 'off the cuff' as it were and told of how Colleen was the person who'd initially convinced him to begin to frequent THE 95. He didn't know whether or not anyone else knew it, but she had bought his meals many times when he'd been less than flush. She also had seen to it that he was kept in aspirin and a multivitamin supplement for old men. He also swore that God would rain down His judgement upon the devil that had done this.

The last person that spoke was Mary, the preacher's wife. She took great care to be humble and admit that God had blessed her with an abundance of resources whereby she was able to become a surrogate mother to Colleen- especially after Wilma had passed on.

David spoke from a few passages in the Holy Bible and he closed out the service by offering everyone present to repeat with him Psalm twenty-three and then the Lord's Prayer. Upon concluding with the benediction, he strode through the crowd of folks shaking hands and accepting the myriad excuses from many for not attending church even though their names were on the rolls. Most of them assured him they would be attending as soon as the weather turned a little warmer. Arthritis just couldn't take the cold of that lofty old building. Or the pews made sister Agnes's legs go to sleep. Brother Francis was mostly deaf and worried his wife, Sally, to death by askin' all the time what the preacher was sayin'. She just couldn't get any listening done for Francis botherin' her during the sermon… so they just quit comin'. But maybe they'd come back soon anyway.

As the mourners disbursed, the tall man that David had noticed hanging behind the crowd-came up to him and took his hand, "I'm Bobby Woodard, Preacher. I was married to Colleen for almost seven years, but I left here nearly three years back. I saw in the paper where she was being buried today and came all the way back here to pay my respects, and to see if she left any instructions about anything she might have left that I could claim for our boy, Eddie. Can you tell me if she ever remarried, or do you know who I might ask about her belongings?"

"Why, yes, Sir. She worked out at THE 95 Truck Stop for a number of years. If anybody can give you any information about her I'm sure those folks would be the ones you'd need to talk with." David took out his handkerchief and wiped his nose, then continued to speak, "And, then you might try talking with the Sheriff." Pointing with his thumb over his shoulder toward the gray-headed man in the tan uniform, he continued. "Sheriff Boyd Custer could tell you just about anything you might need to know, I'm sure." Stepping back, he looked up into the dark eyes of Mister Woodard. "I know you said you saw in the paper about her funeral. How long have you been back in these parts? Did you bring her boy back with you?"

Bobby caught the 'her boy' part, but replied, "I just got in yesterday. I'm stayin' at a motel at 26-95. And no, Eddie's in school and stayed at home with my wife. But, I work with a logging company back home and my boss has asked me to do a little favor for him while I'm here. I just might be here a day or two if that's not gonna' pose a problem for the people around here. I'm sure most of 'em hate my guts for running off with our son and his mama never hearing from me." He looked down at his feet, then back up at David. "I'm sorry for having done it that way, but I couldn't think of an easy way to do it. In hindsight I can understand how losing Eddie nigh killed her. I know if somebody took him from me I'd wanna' kill 'em." With that he stepped back and said, "I'd best be getting' busy tryin' to talk with them about her. Thank you for your time and I wanted to let you know you did a fine job."

David watched the tall man head back toward the dwindling line of vehicles that were parked at the edge of the grass lawn. Then he was taken by surprise when he watched as deputy Raeford went running to try to catch up before he could get away. He could hear the deputy calling after the swiftly moving man.

"Wait up! Hey, wait up Bobby."

Bobby stopped and turned around as Junior caught up with him. "I jes' needed to speak with you a second." He reached to grab Bobby's hand and pumped it. "Sure is good to see you! I've sure missed our rattlin'-great times, man! Whatcha' doin' with yourself now?"

"Been in the lumber business a while. You know I gave up the big highway for loggin? Been hauling for a big company north of here for a while now." They stood apart a few seconds then Bobby spoke, "I need to be getting' outa here. Got an errand to do before it gets too dark." He turned and started for his car, then turned back, "Hey, maybe you can help me. I need to find the office of Trueblood's lumber. Know where it is?"

"Sure. You'll find it off 301 not far beyond Antioch church. It'll be a couple hundred yards up Grassy on the left going out that way. You won't have any trouble. You know the owner? Graham Trueblood? He's a pretty good fella. His girl married my first cousin a couple years back and they already got 'em a set of twin boys! Cute as bugs ears too."

"Thanks, Junior. I'll maybe get together with you for a beer or two before I need to leave."

"Sure thing, Bo." He squeezed the upper arm of Bobby, "Lookin' forward to talkin' over old times!"

CHAPTER 8

Full Moon

LeeRoy was up early. To be honest he had slept very little during the night hours. His mind kept him roving the jungles of Vietnam. He'd been an unofficial sniper for fifteen of those sixteen months. Back then, at the tender age of seventeen, his senses were as keen as they were ever likely to be. It was nothing short of uncanny, his ability – (might I plural that and say instead,) his abilities, as he could smell a cong at a hundred yards. His ears could pick up their underground chatter. Eyes saw booby traps far enough ahead to protect himself, and his buddies as they waded through snake infested muck. Yes. One could surmise that Roy had actually honed his innate skills to a fine scalpel edge by the time his tour was over. The upper echelons decried his loss, but found themselves unable to continue to hold him there. He'd already been there longer than many others. And he had not yet turned into the hardened man-boy who found himself back in Zacchary.

He took up the farm that had literally killed his daddy. Mama had been frozen to settin' and rockin' most days. She contributed as much as possible... shelling peas, snapping beans, peeling or scraping root crops, etc. and etc. And her boy did his best. He'd actually been able to make enough from the hawking of his exceptional crops each Saturday in the local market until he'd assembled a veritable list of paying customers who sought him out and would only buy from him.

Every food morsel possible was dried or canned. Even the peelings, and pickin's were fed to the chickens, from which were gathered daily a number of fat, brown eggs. When there were more available than could be utilized within a few days, the excess was kept in cardboard lids beneath the unused bed in the back bedroom... the bed his daddy died upon.

Frugality became the necessary mistress of their lives, but her stinginess kept the lion of hunger at bay. He and Mae (his mother) became tougher and stringier than lightered knots. Consequently, Mae Hasgrove lived well into her 90s... buried by daddy beneath the big pine, now being lamented by LeeRoy because it'd begun showing signs of beetle infestation. He'd need to take it down before much longer.

He drew on his brown coveralls and heavy boots over the thick wool socks, adjusted the heavy wool mackinaw-camouflaged by the dirt and grime worn into the fibers, so as to greatly resemble the dark bark of some old oak tree. The black knit hat covered his head, face and down his neck. The icy winds and rain would have no power over him this day. Reaching for the compound bow and the loaded quiver he grabbed the tow sack and stepped out into what was left of the night. Another hour and ole' Sol'd be up.

They were heading out to the crime scene, but something told LeeRoy to stop and drop silently to the earth. He wasn't more than a hundred yards away from his shack. Looking back-peering toward the 'feeling', he was rewarded to watch a dark figure bent and blindly, silently, feeling his way around the house. LeeRoy stood slowly, silently, and laid an arrow into the notch and ratcheted back... still aiming at the ground.

The dark figure approached the low porch and stepped up. "You awake, Roy?"

Moving at panther speed, LeeRoy came up behind him and placed his hand on Colonel's back. The scream could be heard all the way to kingdom come! LeeRoy clamped his gloved hand over the open mouth and growled, "Whut th' hell you doin' here this time of night? And why you sneakin' around anyhow?"

"Gawd, Bo! You nigh scared me shitless!" He pulled away and the two entered the warm, dark room.

"Sit. I'll just light a candle for us. Want a cup of coffee?"

"Lord, yes. I ain't thought about getting no coffee or nothing else. But this brain of mine has been beset with all kinds of ideas. I gotta share with somebody to see if anything is worth taking to the sheriff."

"Si'down. I'll brew a pot." He stripped off his head cap and pulled off the mackinaw, tossing it on the unmade bed. "Start blowin' off, Colonel."

Shimmyin' out of the heavy coat, and unwinding the scarf from his head, Chester finally 'harrumphed' his old torso onto the mule eared, straight-backed birch chair. One of the four carved and assembled by LeeRoy's daddy. "Well, first off, what I've been cogitatin' probably ain't worth nuthin' but the knowing of it's about to worry me to death."

After turning on the overhead naked lightbulb, he placed two heavy café-style porcelain cups onto the checkered oilcloth... "It'll be ready in a minute." The heavy shadows danced eerily across the dark wood walls as the two men leaned across the table toward each other. "What's worryin' you so bad 'til it's brought you way out here this time of the morning?"

Nodding, Chester drew in a trembling breath. "I been thinking that it was Bobby what tried to kill our girl, Roy."

Drawing back somewhat, LeeRoy shook his head. "Why you think that? Why he ain't been seen around these parts since he took off with little Eddie. I just doubt he'll ever dare to show up again. He has to know this place would kill him for what he did to Colleen. Nigh destroyed her. Why we all saw how she suffered for her baby. You yourself know she tried to kill herself not a month after they disappeared. If it hadn't been for Milford bein' restless that night and goin' out back for a breath, she'd never have been found in time. As it was, you remember, it was touch and go for a week. She took enough of Jolene's uppers to kill King Kong."

"Yeah, I remember well. Too well. But let me finish why I think it might be him."

"Go on. I'll get the coffee. You take just sugar, don't you?"

"Yeah."

Colonel stirred the spoonful of white crystals into the steaming cup and hovered over it to breath in deeply. "Aaahh! Nectar of the Gods, Roy. I pray God has His brand of French beans in my piece of heaven." Smiling he lifted the thick cup to his lips and blew-sipped enough to burn his tongue exquisitely.

"You were in France during the Allied Occupation." He spoke it as a fact. Not a question.

"Yeah. We boys all thought we'd seen the best life had to offer as we rode through those little narrow streets headin' to Paris. And the girls!! Ain't seen that many willin' females in one pile in all my life! We dogfaces knew we'd arrived!"

Both men smiled at each other. LeeRoy's mind naturally fled to his 'homecoming' from Vietnam. He could still feel the cool spittle upon his young bearded face as it mingled with the tears of hatred for the country he'd nearly died for. His homecoming parade was like being lined up and marched through hell fire. That seared his soul with a feeling he'd carry to his grave. Suddenly jerking himself back to the reality of his kitchen table and the friend across from him, he spoke. "Now, go on, Chester. Talk to me."

"Okay. You do remember him pretty well, don't you?" Not waiting for an answer, he said, "You know he ain't no small man. Six two or three if he's an inch. And you do know he had a scar across his left eyebrow what kinda parted the hairs from growing there." Nodding and taking a slightly deeper sip, he continued, "Well, that ain't something one can very well hide, and so help me God, I've seen him half a dozen times at the ramps. Coming and going in some little gray car. Not his big rig. But never slowing down except when he's held by traffic in front of him. That's when I get to get a good look at him, see? His face don't really look much like Bobby, but with his mustache gone and the sideburns shaved off and his head mostly bald... I swear he needs to be looked into. Reckon you can help me?"

"Well, going by your sightings, I do believe Sheriff Boyd might want someone to investigate this. Did you get the license?"

"Naw. I was so dumbfounded and addlebrained about thinking it was him, until I lost all good sense. No! Damn it. I never did. But I can describe that car. It's too little for his height, but it'll get him to where he wants to be, I guess."

"Okay, Chester. Keep this close for now. Don't say anything to the Sheriff or anyone else. What I suggest you do is git your behind back out there and wait for him to come by again. And get that license number without drawing suspicion as you're doin' it. All right? ... By the way, did he give you a donation?"

"Hell, no. He barely turns his head."

"How is it you can see his eyebrow, then?"

"Now that's a good question, ain't it? Damned if I know, but I'm tellin' you it's there. I've seen it everytime he's driven by, so help me God, Roy! I mean it."

Shoving back his chair, LeeRoy stood. "All right, Chester. Git on back to your palace and see if you can get that tag." Peering out the window at the skyline through the sparsely leaved trees, he saw the sun was coming up quickly. "I gotta get out there fast, or I'll lose the prime hour to get any information." Pulling on the coat and hat, he said, "Stay as long as you like, but cut that light, and close the door snug-like when you leave."

"Thanks, Roy. Can I use your indoor plummin' while I'm here? It'd be a rare treat."

"Sure. The towels and stuff are in a cabinet under the sink. You'll need to let the hot water side run a little bit before it get'll warm. I'll be back within an hour, so I don't wanna find you buck nekkid when I get back! You hear?" He laughed as he stepped out the front door, snugging it closed behind himself.

CHAPTER 9

Rotten News

She awoke to sounds that caused her to scramble from her lounge-chair-bed. Betty quickly snapped on the low bedside light and hovered over her charge within seconds. "My God, Colleen. What's happening?"

Sobbing uncontrollably the patient could not find words. Betty pulled her into a snug embrace and held her for enough time to allow her to begin to calm down. "What did you see? Can you talk about it? Will you tell me?" She reached and snapped on the recorder. "Can you tell me what frightened you, Dear?"

"Oh, Betty. I've never been so scared in all my life. He was going to kill me, and I knew it. I saw his face as he drew the stick up high over me. I remember rolling over and I felt it strike the back of my head. I think he hit me twice." She snubbed and hiccupped and said, "Let me have some water."

"Of course. Here." She held the lidded cup full of icy water up for Colleen to sip. She watched as she drank more than she usually did. "Boy, you're thirsty. Okay?"

Without so much as moving her body, Colleen promptly vomited most of the water out onto the bed, along with vestiges of her supper meal.

"I'm so sorry. So sorry. I didn't know I was going to be sick. I'm so sorry."

Betty rang for help as she began moving Colleen toward standing up and away from the bed cover. "Here, let's get into the bathroom."

"Y'all need help in here?"

"Yes, get the bed changed, please. We had a small accident."

Standing in the bathroom, Betty undressed Colleen, washed her face and wiped off her damp and trembling body. "You think you can void while we're in here?"

"Probably."

While Colleen was seated on the john, Betty found a fresh gown from the closet and went back into the bathroom. She slipped the large printed cotton garment around her and snapped the shoulders closed. "You look like you're freezing to death... just shaking."

"I do feel pretty cold, but I kinda think it's nerves."

They shuffled back into the room, and Colleen watched as Betty and the aide completed the remaking of her bed. "Come on, Honey. Crawl back inside. Let me help you. You still can't use that hand yet. She pulled the blankets over her patient and said, "I swear, he sure did a number on you! It's gonna be a while before you'll have full use of that hand. I think you fought like a real tiger, Honey. Do you know if you were able to injure him in any way? Like scratches to his face, or something?"

"No. I don't know. He was strong and mad and drunk too, I think. His breath smelled like beer. I think he really was just mad at the world and wanted to hurt somebody, and picked me. I guess I was handy. I can remember leaving…"

"Wait. Let me turn it on. Now, go ahead and repeat what you just said."

Okay. Like I was telling you, I think he was mad, and I think he was drunk. At least had been drinking. I think it was beer 'cause his breath smelled just like Bobby's used to when he'd been out drinking. I guess I happened to be in the wrong place at the right time. I know it must have been after I'd gotten off work some few minutes after eleven. I was headed across the parking lot toward my car when he stepped out of nowhere and grabbed my arm. He spoke real soft like and told me he was going to give me a ride home and I tried to pull away, but he was too strong. I started to argue with him, but he clamped his hand over my face and I was having trouble breathing. I think he was choking me. I got panicked and began to struggle, he knocked me with his fist and I felt myself going down.

Betty watched her as her face took on an 'out of body look'. She knew she was living the experience again. "That's enough for right now. Rest a minute or two and let us have a bite to eat before we watch our favorite show. What say?"

Colleen shook her head. "I don't think I'm hungry right now. I still feel kinda sickish. Maybe later."

CHAPTER 10

New Job

Bobby arrived at the office trailer of Graham Trueblood at 7:30 that morning and was glad to see smoke pumping from the small chimney pipe. *Hope he's got some fresh coffee.* And he tapped on the door and opened it right away.

Graham stood with two other burley men next to the little stove. "Come on in, Stranger. Haven't seen you around these parts in many a moon. I saw you couple days ago at Colleen's memorial service out at Oakmont. You are Bobby, aren't you?"

He nodded.

"It's been so long since I've seen you until I wasn't real sure of myself." He leaned over and took Bobby's hand and shook. "I'm Graham Trueblood. What can I do for you?"

One of the two men standing there by the stove, put up a heavily gloved hand and spoke, "Boss, me and Jack's goin on to get to work on that stand.

We'll try to get it finished up for you today." Then nodding to Bobby, they both spoke. "Sorry about your loss, friend." And they shuffled out, slamming the flimsy door behind them.

Bobby figured they must have seen him at the funeral, but why would they assume he'd suffered a loss? *Who are they? I might need to find out.*

"Yes, Mister Trueblood. I hope you can help me."

"Sit down, Bobby."

"Might I have a cup of that coffee? It sure does smell good."

"Why. Of course. Git a cup outa that shelf up there, and the sugar and creamer are there on the stand. Help yourself."

As soon as Bobby had fixed the steaming cup, he sat down in the small straight chair and rocked back on the two rear legs. "I'm on a mission from my boss up in West Virginia. Seems he must know you because he spoke of a contract y'all might have had together. That so?"

"Hummmm. And just who is your boss up in West Virginia?"

"Clifford Bagwell. He owns the Flying Goose Mill. His family has owned that place for three generations. You know him?"

"Oh yeah. I know ole' Cliff. We were classmates back when." He looked kind of far off with a dreamy look in his eyes. "Yes. Indeed, I do know him." He snatched in a quick breath, and said, "And with fondness too. We were in a fraternity together and got ourselves into more trouble than our folks could put up with." He smiled and nodded. "Yeah, I know him." He took a sip of lukewarm coffee. "And he's sent you all the way down here on an errand?"

"Well, not exactly. He probably would've sent his son if I had not already been coming home for Colleen's funeral. I guess that's why he asked me to come see you."

"You said something about some contract I'm supposed to have with him?"

"It's the Cotter property, I suppose."

"Oh Yes! The Cotter property. Prime woods, son. Six hundred fifty acres in it. A small stream staggers right across it from one corner nearly exactly to the other. It's bounded on the west by the railroad tracks, and on the east by 276 for a-ways… then crosses over to hit 301."

He stood and dashed the leftover coffee from his cup into the dirty sink and sloshed a refill back into the gaudy china cup. He took a hefty swig and acted as though it didn't burn his tongue a bit. Bobby was still blowing on his own cup, and thought, *his mouth must be dead.*

"Well, what do I need to do for you and Cliff? I want to be headin' back up country before too long. I left my wife without a car and we live kinda out of the way up the side of a mountain. We do have a telephone though, but if there's an emergency someone would need to drive up there, and we ain't easy to find." He laughed. "We are on a mail route, though!" He smiled broadly.

Nodding his head and grinning, "Got runnin' water?"

"Sure do. All the necessaries." Looking out the dirty window of the flimsy trailer, he continued. "It's beautiful country up there, but the roads can get pretty rough in the winter. Like now. I hate to leave them there alone for too long a time."

"I understand." He sat back down across from Bobby. "Me'n Cliff are bound together… that is our businesses… in an oral contract. We came up with it way back when we first found out we were interested in the same careers. To help each other along, we decided that if either of us was to come upon a really prime piece of timber over five hundred acres, that we'd go 60-40 with the profit." He wiggled his behind in the chair, then stood up and walked over to a front window. "Only twice have we been where we could do this, and both times Cliff found the timber and mailed me my 40 percent. He's stood good to his promise, and I don't know how he found out about the

Cotter land but if you inspect and find it to be prime… which I'm sure it is. Unless it's been riddled with beetles and is hiding too many hardwoods, then I guess I'm on the hook this time to him." Both men were silent and seemed to be lost in thought. Suddenly, Trueblood asked, "When you want to go?"

"As soon as you can give me the plat. Like I said, I really want to get back home as soon as I can."

"Evidently, Cliff trusts you with this or he'd 'a' sent his boy down here. You know Darren?"

"For sure. Darren's been working with his daddy since high school. From all I can gather, he'll be expected to take over the jobs outside of the actual cutting and hauling. I don't know if I'll be let loose or not if he decides to install him as inspector. I don't think there're enough stands available in West Virginia that Cliff'd have access to hold both me and Darren on as inspectors."

"You wouldn't want to let me hire you away from Cliff, now would you?"

"No, sir. I wasn't hinting or anything. Just makin' conversation."

"I understand, but I'm being serious as a judge. I need a man with a quick mind. Able to estimate the output on the run. Someone I can trust with my time, money, equipment and men." He smiled and finished off the coffee before setting the dirty cup into the bottom of the sink. "You think about it while you're out there. I'll match what Cliff's givin' you plus maybe a couple-three thousand a year on top. I don't have the overhead that he does up there in them hills. You'll have good benefits too. I make sure all my employees are taken care of. You think about it."

Taking the rolled plat, Bobby said, "I'll think about it. I'll let you know when I get back this afternoon."

Graham tossed a set of keys to Bobby and said, "Take the truck. It's full and knows the short cuts." He laughed.

"Good. Does Humbert still have that little store out on 301?"

"Sure does."

"Good, I'll pick up lunch to carry with me."

*

"Ashe, listen to me, hon. I think this'd be a good move for us. The job is all lined up for me and its' more money comin' in for us. I think we'd all be happier down here, anyways. What you say?"

"Well, you'd better get on back up here and handle things to get us ready. You know the rent is due for February and he sure won't give you a break if we were to leave today! But, I do think Bobby would probably be more content back down there from here. I think he's too much of a flatlander for these folks. They don't like him much, so I know it'd be better for him. As for me, I'm happy wherever you are, Bobby."

"Good. Then I'll tell Mister Trueblood I'll take the job, if he'll give me a couple of weeks to get us moved."

"Where'll we stay down there, Bobby?"

"Good question. I might look into getting' Colleen's place. But we'll cross that bridge when we come to it. We can hole up in the Marvel for a while. They've got a couple rooms called a suite with a kitchenette and all. We could live there easy until everything's settled."

"When you comin' home?"

"After I settle with Mr. Trueblood about when I'm officially to begin work for him… I'll see him in the morning, and then I'll call you to tell you when to look for me. Okay?"

"Good. I'm anxious to hear from you. You be careful now."

"I will and you too. Take care of Bobby and let him know I love him. Love you too, honey. Bye."

CHAPTER 11

Stressing and Blessing

LeeRoy had only been at home two of the times when Boyd had been out there under the cover of darkness. The State Boys had been spinning their wheels all over town talking to anybody they could get to stand still long enough. Junior had interviewed people to the point of harassment. No one had come close to fingering anyone that could be even considered the guilty person. The two city boys had gone to tell Boyd their office was calling them back since no advancement had been made by then toward the solution. Boyd had begun entertaining the idea that the killer could easily have been someone just passing through. Maybe down 95 and had run up on Colleen in the lot headed to her car that night.

Boyd was glad to see Fred and Horace high tailing it out of town. Good riddance. He felt like he might be able to breathe a little freer with them gone. At least now he didn't have to visit LeeRoy under the cover of darkness. But of course, also, he did not want it spread around that LeeRoy was still very actively engaged in the pursuit of the killer, and so decided to maintain the status quo of the meetings.

LeeRoy had gleaned enough information from his forays into the woods surrounding the place where they'd found Colleen, until he'd told Boyd that as sure as his name was LeeRoy Hasgrove, he'd determined exactly where the killer had dragged her along toward where she was slain.

He'd spent hours peering at the weeds along the rutted road until he came upon tracks where a vehicle had pulled over, crossing the high center, and stopped. There were still vestiges of foot prints-one male boots and the other, female tennis shoes.

The crew at THE 95 had all agreed as to what she'd been wearing that night, and tennis shoes were certainly on that list.

Following the staggering steps which produced the path they took, he could surmise that she was dragged several times. She must have tried to fight him off along the way. LeeRoy could imagine he must have had a vise grip hold on her left hand and how easily he broke the wrist and fingers as they struggled.

He was rewarded several times when he came upon small strands of her white blond hair caught and tangled in low limbs. Once he had the sight of the final assault and rape in his line of vision, he stood and mentally watched the crime being committed. He stood and cried… wept long enough that when he came to himself, he realized it was late, and dark had descended into the woods.

The night was very dark. The moon was in its' three-quarter stage, but the sky was totally overcast, and you couldn't see your hand in front of your face. He made his way back to his home from the crime scene. His cabin was only half a mile away now. *Maybe Boyd'll come by tonight so 's I can bring him up to date on my findings*, he thought.

*

He was sitting at the small table, in the dark silence of contentment, sipping on the last few swallows of tepid coffee left in the cup. His empty tin plate still sat in front of him, along with a can of molasses and one cold biscuit. He finished off the coffee and rose silently. Standing, he envisioned someone headed to his porch. He believed it was the Sheriff, however he maintained his silence. Then he heard the first creak of the lower step. *That's funny. Boyd's never comes up onto the step. He always calls silent like.* He slid his Bowie from his belt and stood where he was, knowing he could not be seen.

The steps sounded as the person walked across the porch toward the door. Then he heard the knob squeak as it was turned. Silently-swiftly-fast as a rattlesnake strike, LeeRoy swung the door open and the man fell into the room. LeeRoy laid the knife against his throat, "Who are you, and what do you want here?"

"Gawd, LeeRoy! It's jes' me. Old Chester."

LeeRoy jerked him up to his feet, "You come close to being old dead Chester tonight!" He dragged him to a chair and sat him down. "I'll lite a candle. Now, tell me why you're sneaking up here?"

"I sure didn't mean any harm, Roy, and honest, I wasn't a-sneakin'. But, I happen to know the Sheriff comes out here right regular, and I just thought maybe he was here with you and so I wanted to see y'all together. I got some news."

"You didn't hear us in here talkin', now did you? So, I ain't buying that you thought the Sheriff was here." He shook his finger in Colonel's face. "Now tell the truth about why you're sneaking up here."

"Well, all right. Truth be told, I was trying to surprise you with a little payback for your kindness to me the other week."

"Kindness? Payback? What you talkin' about?"

"You know. You left me here to get a good bath and get all cleaned up for a change, and I used nigh on to a whole bar of that lemony smellin soap you got. And since it was near gone, I took what little sliver was left, and got ashamed of myself for stealing from such a good friend. Anyway, I went to Lester's and bought you three new bars. I was hoping you'd be out and I could just bring it in and put it away and you'd find it next time you got ready to get your weekly bath."

"Is that a fact?" LeeRoy nodded, "Then where is it?"

Reaching into his heavy jacket, he brought out-first one, then the second one," and felt around for the last of the soap bars. Slapping everywhere there could possibly be a pocket and some places where there couldn't possibly be a pocket, he glanced up at LeeRoy and said, "I've lost it! Somewheres along the way, it musta dropped outa my coat. I swear, I put three bars in this jacket when I left Lester's last night."

"Didn't you pay for them?"

"Well, yes! Yes, I did."

"Then why'd you stick 'em in your pockets when you left there? Why didn't Lester put 'em in a bag?"

"Cause, I told 'im not to… wanted to save him that much."

"I see. Well, I'm satisfied. Go ahead on into the bathroom and stash 'em on the shelf in there. Come on back and I'll fix you a bite to eat. You hungry?"

LeeRoy just didn't have the heart to confess to Colonel that the soap he was so intent on replacing had been sitting there since his mother had died. He, himself would never use it simply because the scent lingered, and he didn't appreciate smelling like a prissy boy. He'd keep it, though, for whenever someone else came by and needed to wash up some. *Lord knows, he can use all the help he can get in that direction.* He smiled at the room, reached up to switch on the light, and blew out the candle in one smooth action.

As Colonel was coming back into the kitchen, he said, "Boy, it sure is nice in here. Cozy like. Colder'n a welldiggers behind out there tonight." Barely drawing a breath, he continued, "Sure it's not too much trouble to stir a vittle for me?"

"Nah. Eggs and a biscuit and some molasses'll do, won't it?"

Sitting at the table, he dumped a mounded spoon of sugar into the cup as LeeRoy poured the bubbling hot coffee into it. Glancing up at his friend, he said, "You know, Roy… I got more news."

"Wonderin' when you'd come around to the real reason." He laughed. "I know you Chester. If you can drag out your visit, you're sure to get fed or bathed! Now, ain't that a fact?"

Laughing too. "Guess we've been at it long enough to have no secrets, eh, Roy."

Setting the plate of scrambled eggs before his guest, he said, "Sorry, the biscuit is cold, but it'll still sop molasses."

"Roy, this is food for the gods, son. Best food in this world is plain and plentiful. Satisfyin' to my soul. And I thank you."

While Chester was busy eating, Roy cleaned his dishes and stacked the few items off to the side of the sink on a discolored wire rack to drain. Coming back to the table, he asked, "When've you seen any activity from Junior in the way of delving to try to solve our murder?"

"Hurumph! Junior ain't doin' nothin' that any of us can see to even try to make any headway. I think you must really be the only one active. I don't even think Sheriff Boyd is doin' much. We never see him out at THE 95 anymore."

"You serious?"

"But let me tell you who we see all the time out there."

"Who is that?"

"Her ex. That's who. Let me tell you, I think he ain't plannin' to go back to where he was. That bother's me some. Begs the question as to where her boy is!" Chester leaned back and contentedly sipped his coffee.

LeeRoy cleared the table and wiped what few crumbs there were. "Why you say he ain't plannin' to leave here?"

"Well, he came for the funeral two weeks back, and he's still here. I'm thinking he's done got rid of the boy and back here to see what she might have left unclaimed."

"Then you keep your antennae up high, and your rattletrap shut. Maybe you'll come up on some good ideas for us to investigate. Okay?"

"Sure, Roy. I'll do my best. It's just that he don't seem to say much. Sit's and listens mostly. Eats his meal, and'll mosey on. I do think he's out at the Marvel, though. I heard him offer some hitchhiker a ride that far, so I figured that's where he's stayin' for the time being."

"We'll need to look into it."

"You don't suppose he did her in first, then come showing up here to her funeral to make everyone believe he'd just got into town, do you?"

"You just might have something there, Colonel. I'll put that bug in Boyd's ear unless you want to."

"Nah. You do it. You'll see him before me anyway." Rising from the chair and gently placing it under the table neatly, he said, "I thank you friend for your hospitality. I'll be headin' out now."

"Can I drive you back? I'd be happy to. I like the company, and besides I need to go see if I can glean some info from some of the joints that are still open."

"Sure! I'd be much obliged."

*

Roy pulled off the highway beneath the overpass that Colonel called home… far enough to be out of the line of traffic and let Chester out. "Nite, man."

Waving, he returned, "Nite, Roy, and thanks for supper."

"Thanks for the soap," as he drove off up 95 toward any bustling nightlife he might come upon.

CHAPTER 12

Homecoming

At dusk, the little family pulled into the parking area of the Marvel Motel at the intersection of 26 and 95 – where Bobby had been staying earlier. He'd procured a suite for his wife and boy and they began offloading the overloaded vehicle. The big rented trailer was left unopened until they could find a house. They were dead tired and so ate their supper from the leavings of the large brown bag which that morning Ashe had loaded with sandwiches and snacks. They never stopped except to 'gas up' and rest a couple times along the way. They were all anxious to get back to what they all perceived to be 'a better existence' down south.

The mountains were wonderfully beautiful, but harsh on the living for those not raised in them. They'd been blessed by the landlord magnanimously returning half the rental money for February. After all, he'd already received a down payment from a wounded veteran wanting to rent the place to 'get away from the world' and thought that was it.

*

Within a week-by Feb fifteenth, Eddie had been installed into the third grade of a private school at Summerton. They had talked it over, and since there was such a mystery that would invade the life of Eddie, they determined that he'd have a better chance in a private school. "You know. Be more protected," Bobby had argued. With the cost of this option, Ashe knew she'd surely need to find a job somewhere to help with the expenses until they could finally settle down somewhere and get their budget worked out.

Before the day was out, Ashe had procured a job as Hostess at C&S Golf Course outside of Zacchary. A job she was sure she could easily handle and become a real asset to the owner. She brought out her most business-like clothes, and polished the only pair of low-heeled pumps she owned. They didn't look bad, she surmised.

When she arrived for her first morning of work, David Zimmerman-owner, met her at the desk, and was pleasantly surprised by her air of efficiency. "I think you're gonna' work out real well here. But, come now, and let me show you all around the place and introduce you to your cohorts." He smiled. Reminding Ashe of some alligator. She reminded herself to be on her guard at all times. She just might need to put him in his place, even at the risk of losing this job.

*

While attempting to find a home for his family, Bobby had been warned away from Colleen's house by the sheriff. When Bobby had gone by there to check it out he saw it was still off limits and wound around the perimeter was the yellow crime tape. He'd promptly sought out Boyd to inquire as to why the place was still unopened.

"That tape'll stay up around the place until we find her killer. I don't want any would be evidence messed up by folks traipsin' through there."

"Boyd, I understand all that, and appreciate all you're tryin' to do to catch the devil that did this to Eddie's mama. But me and Ashe and Eddie now are moved back down here, and I've got a good job with Trueblood. I need a house to move my family in to. You happen to know of anything decent where we can rent?"

Taking the hat off his balding gray head, he said, "Let me see. Widow Clark might still want someone to live in her house and kinda look out for her for rent. You might want to see if Ashe and Eddie could stand living in with the old woman. I think she's pretty even tempered but that'd be up to y'all. Then of course, there's William's Trailer Park out up 301 a-ways. His trailers are always pretty clean."

"Are the trailers furnished?"

"Now, that I don't know."

"When you spoke of a Mrs. Clark, I figured she must have plenty of furniture already, and Ashe and I have brought our furniture down with us. It's still stashed in a hauler out at the motel. I'd kinda like to find a small house- maybe even a duplex, to rent for the time being, since we've plenty of furniture already. Only thing we'd need would be a cook stove and refrigerator. We already have a washer and dryer."

"You suit yourself. But before you waste much effort, if I was you I'd talk with your wife about goin' to talk with Mrs. Clark. I bet she'd let you move most of your stuff in there. Her house is plenty big. She'd probably have enough room for ten families to move in." He grinned.

"Okay, Boyd. Thanks. I'll be getting on over to Trueblood's. I appreciate your kindness."

"You're welcome, Bobby. Glad you're back, but try to stay away from Junior. You two are like a house fire when y'all are together. I know your new wife won't appreciate you actin' up like you used to do when you were married to Colleen."

"Yes'sir. I recall our recklessness back then. But, I have to say I've changed and I pray that Junior has too."

*

"Mrs. Clark? This is Ashe Woodard calling. Sheriff Custer told me you may like to have a small family to stay in your home. Is this true?"

"Why, yes. You say your name's Ashe Woodard?"

"Yes ma'am. I married Bobby Woodard after he and Colleen broke up. We've been married something over two years."

"Well, that's nice. And to answer your question; Yes, I would very much like to have a young family to live in with me to help me around here and I'd feel much safer too… in this big ole' house."

"That sounds good, ma'am. Could I maybe come 'round to visit with you to see if we'd be compatible? We have a nine-year old son, and he can be a handful, if you know what I mean. I wouldn't want you to be uncomfortable with having a rambunctious young'un under your feet."

"He sounds like he might keep me on my toes!" She laughed. "Would you like to come over today? I've already finished dinner and Tilda left about ten minutes ago."

"Certainly. I must close out here then and run to pick up Eddie. I'll need to bring him with me, if that's all right."

"Oh, that would be fine. We'd get to meet each other that way before we make our decisions. Could you be here before six?"

"I think so. Unless something unforeseen arises. If it does, then I'll call you as soon as I know. All right?"

"That's fine, dear. And, tell me what kind of car will you be driving? I don't ever go to the door unless I know who is out there, you understand?"

"Yes, I do. I will be driving a small gray Ford Focus car."

"Very good, dear, I'll be looking for you, then."

CHAPTER 13

Breakdown

Junior had kept himself busy with all the 'errands' suggested by his boss, Sheriff Boyd. He'd been a nuisance out at THE 95 Restaurant lately. Not only in everyone's way – especially bothersome to Jolene as he attempted to impress her with his keen intellect… loudly spouting about the advancements being made on solving the murder.

Customers initially were enthralled, but soon saw through his blustering's, and turned aside to try to enjoy their food in peace.

Seasoned truckers smiled knowingly at each other and one was overheard to whisper, "Don't know his ass from a hole in th' ground!" The table guffawed loudly while Junior's face shown crimson and the back of his neck burned. He stalked loudly out, slamming the door.

I'll show them damn devils! They done messed with Junior once too often, he thought. "Think I'll go find Bobby," he muttered under his breath.

The light from a half moon shown down on his white cruiser as he headed out to The Marvel. Pulling into the parking lot with a screech of tires, he slammed out of the vehicle and headed to the office. "Where's Bobby Woodard's room? Police business."

"He ain't here right now, Junior. Him and his little family are out somewhere. Probably getting' supper or something."

"Give me his room number for later on. I won't bother you."

"Sure. They've got our best suite. It's around on the south side, number 12. On the corner."

"I ain't dumb, Sam. I can read! I'll find it." He attempted to 'slam' out of the glass doors, but they were fixed with vacuum closers and this set up another round of discontent.

Slinging the cruiser out of the lot, was the beginning of the end, for Junior... at least for the time being. A nearly full bottle of Jack Daniel black, slid out from beneath the seat. Upon spying the bottle, he salivated, and a small trigger snapped in his brain. *Gawd! How long's this been in here? Just what I'm needin' tonight to get me through this mess.* Pulling off the highway onto a side road, he sped on until he found what he was searching for... a farmer's access road to some pasture or other. He pulled into the close bushes surrounding the nearly non-existent road, literally tore off the screw lid, and turned up the fine whiskey. Heaven! Stopping to breathe was not necessary. His nostrils flared as he drew breath after breath between gulps. Careful not to waste a drop. Within just a few seconds the square bottle was empty. He rolled down the window and pitched it out, along with the cap.

He sat and belched. Looking out the window into the halfmoon night he was greeted with visions of the mangled body of the woman he'd been in love with ever since high school. At that point he hated Bobby for bringing about the horrible events of last month. She'd chosen Bobby over him, and then

Bobby had run out on her. Not just that but had stolen her little boy. Ever since her damn man had run off-three long years he'd been there, begging silently to be noticed. Always ready to see her home in the dead of night. Offering to carry whatever needed carrying. Three long years she hadn't given him the time of day. Three long years he carried a hard for her body. And then it was too late. She was dead.

He slumped over the wheel and sobbed. Why hadn't she picked him? Why couldn't she see that he loved her? Why didn't she understand he'd do anything in the world for her? He loved her. He loved her. He loved her. *I'll go see her right now. I'll tell her again how much I love her.*

Backing out of the road and turning back toward town and the Oakmont Cemetery, he suddenly thought better of possibly being seen crying at her grave. *I'll head in to see about finishing up those reports. God! Why does Boyd always insist on having that damn stuff done every day! He's such a damn slave driver. I hate his guts. One of these days I'll just show him! I'll beat the shit out of his ugly face!*

By the time he returned to the complex, he was fuming. Kicking at the benign stones that edged the paved walk, his temper was on high alert. By this time of night, the skeleton crew of probably no more than two, were the only ones in the building-not that he'd given it any consideration.

Banging his fist upon the glass doors, and kicking at the center, he was soon rewarded with watching Ski running toward him. "What's the hell's matter with you? Why'n'chu ring the damn buzzer? Idiot! Surely to God you ain't drunk, Junior!" Pressing the inside switch which caused the door to swing open, Murdock Murkowski stepped back and allowed Junior to stumble into the dimly lit entry way. "Now e'zakly what's your dander up about this time?" He followed Junior as he stomped out into the office complex. He could smell the liquor from ten feet away. "You need a woman to go home to, Junior. Somebody to keep yore ass straight."

Ski continued to follow, and watch, hoping for an opportunity to see him begin to simmer down.

"Yeah! But my little woman is dead! Dead as hell, Ski! Dead. Some sonabitch took her beautiful body out of this world." He slumped down at the desk of Sheriff Custer, and swung around in the chair. Suddenly, he swiped the desk top clean with his long arm. Sent papers, telephones, files, pens, scissors, and all attendant paraphernalia flying in a scattering across the crowded room.

Ski tore back to his desk in the other end of the divided spaces and grabbed his phone. Punched a button or two, waited a second or two, then, "Git down here now, Sheriff! Junior's done gone crazy agin'. Come armed. He's still in uniform, so you know what that means. Hurry."

From the other end of the line, "Alert Sidney to come fast. He needs to be locked up, but you're might gonna need my help disarming him first. I'm on my way."

By the time Ski was headed back to the Sheriff's office he spied Junior drunkenly stalking down the corridors, peering into every lit office to find it empty, he slammed off the lights that had been left on. Hollering at the top of his lungs, "Dumb Asses! Cain't keep a simple light switch turned off!" He ended up in the back where cellmates were laughing and slapping cards at each other as they enjoyed their game in the common room. "What th' hell is goin' on here?" Junior demanded.

Jumping up Teddy and Washington sputtered, "Why nothin', Junior. Ain't nothin' goin' on. We're just playing Twenty-one is all."

"Well, git to bed. Past time for light's out." And he swung back toward Ski. "Are you followin' me? What for? You skeered I'm gonna do something to upset somebody?" He shoved Ski aside as he headed back to the offices.

Upon feeling the jail door suck/slam behind him, Ski hurried to catch up with Junior, "Come on into my cubby. I'll fix you a cup of coffee. Okay?"

By this time Junior was glassy eyed and slobbering. His nose was dripping from his earlier crying. "I'll do that, Ski. Here, help me set down. I feel like I'm gonna fall."

The two reeled together toward the second cubby ahead, and Ski was able to get him down into a low chair in front of his desk. "Stay. I'll get the coffee."

When Ski returned with the steaming coffee in an old, stained, 'community cup', Junior was snoring upon the cement floor. He placed the cup on his desk and ran out to meet Sheriff Boyd just coming in the building from the back entrance.

"What's the status of our boy?"

"Pretty good right now. He's asleep in my office… on the floor."

"This is getting' bad, Ski. I thought he had beaten it, but I guess I was wrong. Second time now since the turn of the year. Come on, let's see if we can disarm him before he wakes. Soon's Sidney gets here we can lock 'im up for the night. That ought to hold 'im until we can get him to the doctor sometime tomorrow. I'll need to put him on leave until he can get hisself straightened out."

CHAPTER 14

Tunnel Ahead

Next morning Boyd found himself letting Junior out of the cell he'd occupied from where he'd been locked in from the wild night just past.

"Wash your face and come on into my office."

Within a few minutes, the disheveled deputy slouched into the chair in front of the desk. "I wasn't bad enough for y'all to throw me in a cell! You could'a just sent me on home.

Boyd sat forward and gazed at the younger man with a deadly glint in his eyes. "Shut up and hear what I'm commanding will happen this day."

For the next few minutes Junior sat in sullen silence, until his mind began to absorb the serious nature of the words coming from his superior…

"Naw, Boyd… Boss!" Shaking his head. "Man! Naw. Don't send me out there. I'll be all right, I promise. You know I can do it if I put my mind to it.

Sir, I don't need to go. Really. I'll beat it by myself like last time. Didn't I tell you and didn't I do it?"

Agreeing with him for expediency's sake… "Yep. You did. But I'm seeing to it that this time we're going the proper route to get this taken care of once, and for all." He paused and peered at his deputy. "Of course, you can deny this request and refuse to sign yourself into the facility. But, if you don't go willingly, then I have nothing left but to suspend you without pay until you do see the need to go. If that fails, then you'll be fired. And you know you'll never be in law enforcement again. You understand me?"

Junior slumped in the chair, and bowed his head and nodded slowly. "Okay. I'll turn myself in to Doctor Tillage first thing tomorrow."

"Unh uh. No. And it won't be Tillage. You'll do it this morning. I've already spoken with Director Peters up there. He's got your bed ready… you can have your lunch at 'Hope House' today. All's you need is the clothes on your back. They'll supply the uniforms, robes and flipflops, and all the necessities. You ain't even gonna need a new toothbrush, son."

Peering up at his boss, Junior said, "Looks like you wanna get rid of me. Is that right?"

"Yes! I need you to get well and get back here as soon as you can. But for me to rely on you, son, I gotta know you can stay straight. You're the best when you're at your best. It's as simple as that."

"Guess it's time for me to put up or shut up. Right?" Junior stood, and the two men walked out to the foyer of the complex where they stopped. Junior stooped a little and looked out front. "Pretty sure of yourself, ain't you. Already got Twisted Britches out there warming up the car."

Quickly, Boyd reached and hugged the younger man. "Now git on up there so you can git back here and help us solve this murder!"

Oh, Lord. Why'd he have to say that? Lord, help me. He ran out the door and jumped into the front of the cruiser being driven by their youngest deputy.

CHAPTER 15

Checking It Out

Ashe and Eddie stepped up onto the wide porch and walked to the massive double doors, inlaid with stained glass. Ashe reached down and straightened the boy's shirt and wiped his hair with her hand. She then pressed the elaborate button on the right side of the door, to hear the beautiful chimes from somewhere within the mansion. The two visitors stepped back a couple of feet to wait. They were rewarded forthwith by an elderly black man in simple attire.

"Might I help you, Ma'am?"

"Yes. I'm Mrs. Ashe Woodard and this is my son, Eddie. We're here to see Mrs. Clark. She's expecting us, I believe."

Swinging the right door inward, he said, "Yes, Ma'am. Come on in. Missus Clark is in the den. It's a little warmer in there. Just follow me."

The trio stepped off to the left of the large, open, marbled-floored, stair-swept central foyer and entered a carpeted hallway. Ashe was struck by the richness of the interior of the home. It more than mirrored the expanse and magnificence of the exterior. The hall was wide and accommodating-paneled in what appeared to be beaded mahogany wainscoting with dark wallpaper in some sort of large design up to the high ceiling. She breathed deeply to inhale the comforting scent of lemon wax mingled with something akin to a cedar odor. She mentally shook her head at the luxurious surroundings, musing how some folks had it all.

As they neared the den, they were all aware of the sound of a blaring television from inside. The black man knocked once upon the door and opened it. He strode in and lifted the remote control and turned the television off. Going to the lady, he leaned down and spoke loudly, "Mrs. Clark! Your company is here Ma'am! Missus Clark!"

"Oh, I'm awake Jefferson! I'm awake. I was only resting my eyes." She smiled at him and he smiled back, "Yes'sum. Yo company's here, Ma'am."

He turned and seated Ashe upon the settee with Eddie next to her. "I'll leave you now, unless you need me for anything else?"

"No, thank you." As he was turning to leave, she quickly asked, "Oh! Before you go, please add a couple more logs to the fire. Then you can go."

Once that had been accomplished, he left and the three sat a few moments assessing each other. Mrs. Adelaide Clark thought: *Seems to be a right pretty lady and the boy appears well kept. Says a lot about a mother taking care of herself and her child.*

She appears to very astute and full of mischief. Hope she like us. I'd love living in this place. Wonder where she'd put us? Thought Ashe.

Boy! If I lived here couldn't nobody say I was second class! No Sir! I sure hope we can be livin' in this big ole' place. And Eddie's eyes were big as saucers as he glanced around the room.

"Would you care for some refreshment, dear?"

"No, thank you, Mrs. Clark. Eddie and I are fine. We'll need to fix supper after we leave here. I don't want to ruin our appetites. But thank you for the offer."

"I suppose you want to ask me questions about what the arrangements might be if you were to move into my home?"

"Of course."

"Ask away, dear."

"Yes ma'am." Ashe settled with a little wiggle and leaned forward toward the elderly lady, "Mrs. Clark, we have a good deal of our own furniture. Would it be feasible for us to move it into your home?" Then quickly, "That is… IF we decide it's best for you as well as for us."

"I understand, my child. Yes. Your family would be given four of the upstairs rooms. There's a small kitchenette with a dining table there. And just across the hall is a full bathroom between two bedrooms. Then there's a fairly, good sized sitting room there too. Most of the rooms are empty except that I do have a small refrigerator and an apartment size gas stove for the kitchen. Your apartment will have its own gas water heater… separate from downstairs. You would need to be responsible for the gas and electric bill as the apartment is on a separate line." She stood and stoked the fire and pitched on another small log. "Would you like to see it?"

"Later, perhaps. But I need to know how much it will cost per month for us to stay here. Have you thought about that?"

"Oh, my dear. I was hoping you'd help me out by seeing to my safety and helping with my laundry when you are doing yours… and my grocery shopping. I already have Jefferson who takes care of the yards and chopping wood, and things like that. Then there's Tilda who comes in and cooks my dinner meal, cleans the kitchen and leaves. The house never really gets swept or dusted, nor the windows washed. And, I am always scared every time I get ready to take a bath, so I've just taken to bathing off at the sink. I feel that I never really get good and clean. Do you see my quandary? I'd so very much appreciate your help with little things like seeing that I have your attendance for those times when I'm afraid for myself. Do you understand?"

"Of course, I do. And, I'd be more than happy to help you in any way possible. But, I do have a job to keep so I could only be available before work and after work."

"I am certain that I would be able to reconcile my needs to your schedule, dear. I do understand how important your position is within your sweet family, and I'm sure your job is an absolute necessity. Particularly nowadays. Everything is so high, and wages are so low until this has caused many a mother to join the work force." She smiled benignly, and then continued. "No, dear. The rental fee would certainly be waived in our case. As I said, all you'd be responsible for would be the gas and electric bill. The water comes from a deep well which has never given one iota of trouble. Even in the driest or wettest of times. The water is always pure, clear and easily potable."

"Do you honestly tell me that we'd not be responsible for rent?"

"Yes. That's what I've decided. If you can simply help me do the things that I find myself now incapable of accomplishing, it would be worth the rental fee twice over, I'm sure."

"Without wasting your time, I shall contract with you for the use of your four upstairs rooms then. However, I'd love to see them when you feel up to taking me upstairs. And, too, is there an outside entrance?"

"No. There's no outside stairway, but the stairway off the downstairs kitchen would be the easiest route for you. You all could park at the back door carport, and leave your car there. I'd give you a key to that door, but you'd need to promise me that you'll always keep it locked whether you're here or not. I usually let Jefferson and Tilda come in that way to bring wood or whatever else and I keep the side and the front doors locked. "

Standing, Ashe reached out to take the hand of Mrs. Clark. "Thank you for your graciousness to me and to Eddie. We appreciate your kindness. Since it's getting late, we must be running along now, but I'd like to come by at your convenience to view the rooms before we begin bringing our furniture, if that's all right."

"Anytime tomorrow will be all right. Just call first so I will know to expect you." She began walking toward the front hall, but stopped and reached out for Ashe, "But, Dear, if you find you have need of a piece of furniture, please do not go out and buy it. Just head into the attic. The stairway is at the other end of the hallway when you come up from the first to the second floor. The attic has all the furniture that was taken from the rooms you'll be using." She began walking again. "You see, my niece and her husband moved in here right after they eloped. They had six months together before he was sent to Viet Nam. He was killed there, and Sylvia left soon after for somewhere. I never heard from her again."

Stopping to sadly shake her gray head… "You see, her parents were killed just after the time she'd met and fallen in love with Thomas. They had not approved of her choice, so those children eloped. The next day she found herself and orphan-my sister and her husband died in a terrible accident while on vacation up in the mountains. They didn't even know their only child was married." She breathed in a tremulous breath. "I happened to be her only relative, and so she brought Thomas and came to me. I believe they had a good marriage. Thomas was her wellspring during those days of mourning as well as helping her adjust to becoming a wife. After her husband left for Vietnam, we put her parent's house up for sale and it was sold about the time she learned that Thomas had been killed." She stood with a faraway look in her eyes.

The trio were standing in the large foyer. Mrs. Clark looked toward the rounding staircase and then continued, "I remember seeing her coming down those stairs with her bags packed. I was standing about where I am now. I could see the tears streaming down her cheeks. She walked over to me and took her time to place her arms around me. I can even feel that hug now." Ashe was holding Adelaide's frail hand. "I can still feel the warmth of her breath. Her words – 'I love you Auntie, but I've got to go. You'll hear from me, I promise.' But, I never did. I don't know what happened to the child. I've often wondered…"

Ashe leaned down to place her arms around the little lady, and kissed the soft cheek. "I'm so very sorry. Maybe one day you'll hear from her." Standing back upright, she took Eddie's hand and reached to open the front door. "Good bye for now. I'll call tomorrow."

CHAPTER 16

Unexpected Expecting

Betty rolled her distraught patient back into the room and helped her pile back into the bed. "What're you going to do, Hon?"

"Oh, Betty. This is the worst thing ever!" She sobbed. "I wanted another child before Bobby ran off, but I thanked God I wasn't pregnant when he left. And now this!" She sobbed in body-wracking wails.

"Well, the OB Doctor advised you to terminate. That would take care of any problem that could arise from this pregnancy."

"I know, I know. But I just don't believe I can murder an innocent baby no matter how it was conceived."

"You've got a little while before you need to make the decision. I'd advise you to talk with the Chaplain. He'll might be of some help to you, I'm sure. Want me to send for him? He's usually here during the week around supper time and after. He'd be happy to help you."

"Maybe that'd be best." Colleen snubbed some, and then blew her nose and wiped it. "I'll make the decision after I've talked with him." Settling herself into the nest of her bed, she said, "Get the recorder. I feel like talking, and I think I might come up with more memories of the attack."

"Know who it was, yet?"

She shook her head. "I recall seeing his face, but it was dark, and he looked mad… you know, like some demon. I gotta say he even favored Bobby some. Same size and smell, if you know what I mean."

"Great. Here, let's turn it on." Betty said, "It's four fifteen the afternoon of February 16th in the room of Colleen Woodard. Now, just take your time, relax and talk of whatever comes into your head."

"After he'd knocked me out in the parking lot, I assume he put me in a truck… you know, the kind with the tall tires. All the hunters seem to have them. The reason I think it had tall tires is because I woke up while we were bouncing across deep ruts and through bushes. I could feel the bouncing and hear the stuff scraping against the sides of the truck. I remember my hand was hurting so much. I tried to move it, but I couldn't, I think he may have tied me up before he put me in there. I'm sure I must have been lying on the floor in the back between the front and rear seats. The transmission hump was killing my back. I listened to see if I could hear anything to identify where we might be. Nothing; except I did hear an owl a couple of times, so I figured we were in some woods somewhere. From where I was laying, I couldn't see any light through the windows. I think it must have been cloudy or the moon was not up. After what seemed like an hour… I really don't believe it was that long. I was hurting something awful. My head was pounding, and I think I kept going to sleep. I don't recall him ever talking to me. I guess maybe I might've known him if I'd heard him speak in a regular voice. At the parking lot, he sounded so drunk and talked with whispers and in a throaty and guttural voice.

I don't know if that was on purpose or not. But, I kept thinking he was big. You know big like Bobby. Not fat." She stopped and reached for the water. "Think I'll risk a sip. Maybe I can keep it down."

She smiled sadly, and began again. "Once the truck stopped, he opened the door and dragged me out by my feet. My body and head struck the foot step and he literally dumped me upon the ground. I felt stiff grass, and smelled the dankness of nearby woods… you know, rotting leaves of heavy hardwoods. I kept my eyes closed. Maybe on purpose, or else I kept passing out. I remember being so cold and felt myself being dragged. He never carried me. He just dragged me. Over fallen trees, through bushes and one time he had to tear the briars out of my hair to get me loose. I was almost relieved when he pulled me to where I knew he planned to kill me. I remember looking up, but in the dark, all I could see was a quick shimmer of an open knife. I could feel him cutting my clothing. That must have been when he sliced open my legs as he sawed at my jeans to get them off. I heard the fabric of my blouse being torn and jerked away. And then I saw the heavy stick raised up and coming down. I turned quickly over and felt him strike the back of my head. Twice. The next thing I recall is when I was able to get my eyes open, and saw flashlights and them running the toward me. I was embarrassed to know I was naked."

Betty reached over and flipped the switch off. "This latest just might give our boys something to go on." She stood, "I'm going to go put in the request for Reverend Dawson to stop by when he gets here this evening. Now you rest. They'll bring your evening snack in a few minutes. Don't eat until I get back, Okay? I want to be with you when you eat."

Colleen smiled, slid down into the comfort of the bed, and dropped off to sleep. She could hear Betty's voice within her dream and felt happy about him not coming until the morning.

"Rev Dawson is comforting a grieving family tonight. He'll be in to see you in the morning, if that's ok." Betty leaned over the bed and saw the smooth even breaths of the sleeping woman. "You sleep on, dear. All will be well before much longer."

CHAPTER 17

Dug Up Evidence

"He parked here, Boss, then you can still see where she was dragged out through here."

The two men made their way through the tall weeds and entered the woods that were mostly hardwoods, in this particular area.

Boyd shook his head as he reached and pulled some glistening white hairs from the loosened bark of a fallen log. "My God, Roy! He must'a thought she was already dead to drag that poor girl like this."

"Yeah, else he was too drunk to know what th' hell he wuz doin'."

They picked their way on toward the yellow tape in the distance.

"Must be couple hundred yards to where they left the vehicle." Boyd was silent for a few seconds, then said, "I believe our victim was mistaken about the vehicle she was transported in. You know she told us she thought he'd put her in the back seat of a high-wheeled truck. I think she must have been totally out of it, as what I saw back yonder are tracks from a smaller pickup. Something lighter weight. Maybe a real old one or a later model foreign one. What you think?"

"I'd have to agree. But from the tires I think you're dealing with an older American made truck. Maybe something that was used on a farm, as I smelled manure around where it was parked."

"Wow! Roy. I'm grateful for your sense of smell. Anything else you know that I need to know?"

"I think the boots he wore were a smidgin too large for his feet, and he left the odor of garbage on the ground around where the rape and murder took place."

"Wonder what he did with those boots and the clothes she was wearing. She was so torn up, until I think he must'a literally tore 'em off of her… probably used a knife to help rip them off too. I know Hatfield had to stitch up her legs where she'd been cut pretty bad."

Shaking his head, he held the tape up for Roy to sweep beneath, then the two minced steps over to where the terrible deed had been accomplished. Leaning down to point to a certain place, Roy looked up at Boyd, "This was where he stood over her. See how his foot prints are spread? You can tell the boots were either too big, or else weren't laced and tied. See here. The outside of the soles dug deeper into the earth. That tells me his feet inside were slipping toward the outer edge inside the boot."

Moving around the area, Roy stopped again, "Here's where his knees straddled her body as he raped her. The pants he'd pulled down were never taken all way off. They were down around his calves. Here's where the belt buckle pressed into the dirt. I had to sweep away a few leaves, but I found it. If you look close you can see an initial."

"What is it?"

"R."

"Robert?"

"Could be anybody. I wore my daddy's hand-me-downs and it could be the same with this. This may or may not be important, but it gives you one more scrap of evidence.

"See anything else?"

"Not much. Of course, her hair is everywhere. Her fingernails could have plenty of dirt. And there's the possibility she got some good swipes on him when she wasn't out cold. Those two city slickers dug up a fair amount of the dirt where she bled into the ground too. But, I guess you have all that."

"Yeah." Raising back upright, Boyd asked, "Now Bo, can you figure out how he left out of here?"

"Sure can. You see, he never went back to the truck then. He took off across here." Roy stepped around the big oak and pointed toward an area where the hardwoods thinned, and the pines thickened. "Come on. I'll show you."

Boyd followed shaking his head in disbelief. They walked for quite a long while, with Roy periodically slowing to get his bearings on the trail. Suddenly he stopped. Boyd figured they must be close to about half a mile from the crime scene. Standing stock still and holding his hand back for Boyd to follow suit, Roy motioned for silence.

They were soon rewarded to observe Bobby strolling through the pines a hundred yards or so ahead. They silently watched as he would stop, lean in toward the bark of a tree and flick a chunk of bark off. He'd smell it, drop it and search around as he stepped on. They kept moving up little by little to keep him in their sight. Bobby moved on out of the pines and into an overgrown area… the yard of an old rotting cabin surrounded by gnarled apple trees and bare, overgrown plums bushes.

"The old Cotter homeplace," whispered Boyd. "Looks like he's working. You can barely see Truebloods' truck parked around on the far side. I'd heard he'd been hired on as an inspector for Graham."

"Let's stay out'a sight, Boyd. I don't want anybody to know we've gotten this far tracking our killer. After he leaves we can see whether or not our trail plays out here, or what."

"Hope he isn't here too long. I need to pee something awful."

"Better hold it down as close to the dirt as possible. And for God's sake, don't fart!" Admonished Roy.

Boyd knelt down, and quietly unzipped his trousers and worked his penis out and held it downward close to the dead leaves.

"Here, wipe them leaves out'a the way first."

Swiping at the dead leaves to open a spot of black earth, he let loose and soon had the urine flooding out beneath the covering of surrounding leaves. Not much noise was made, that wasn't covered by the natural soughing of the pine forest.

Both men squatted together to watch Bobby as he opened a brown sack and began eating something. About that time a half-starved cur rounded the house and wagged his body as he cowered closer to the scent of food. Bobby tore off half his sandwich and hand fed it to the animal. Reaching out he stroked its head. Then fed the remainder of his food to the canine. They could hear Bobby's speech as he told the dog it was all gone. The beggar seemed to understand and wandered off, sniffing like a blood hound. Bobby watched its' antics as he drank the remainder of the canned Pepsi. Stuffing the can into the brown sack he crushed them together and pitched it in the direction of the dog. He stretched and stood up to observe the dog industriously digging at an area about twenty feet away from where he stood. Soon the dog dragged a piece of fabric from the earth and ran with it over to his provider. Wagging his tail, he dropped it upon the earth at Bobby's feet. "What'chu got there, Spike?" He reached down and picked it up. "You done found yourself a genuine ladies handkerchief." Dropping it back onto the earth, he said, "Want to go home with me? I bet my little boy'd love to have you to take care of. Come on. If you can git in the truck without my help, then I'll take it that your answer is 'yes'. Okay?"

Bobby walked around to the other side of the dilapidated cabin, followed closely by the small dog. The two men could hear him congratulating Spike upon successfully leaping into the cab. They heard the engine crank, and watched as the truck pulled out of sight and then back into sight as it bounced across the rutted, roadless, expanse of weeds toward the narrow, hidden road which led back to the dirt road about half a mile from where they stood.

Without a word, Boyd and LeeRoy ran to the place where the dog had dug up the handkerchief. They were soon uncovering the cut and torn clothing of Colleen as well as a full set of men's clothes.

"I don't think our killer is Bobby."

"Why not?"

"Well, he'd never have let that dog get at them clothes and sure as hell wouldn't a throwed that handkerchief back on the ground like he did."

"Son. I've seen near everything in my years. He could'a been so drunk and out of his mind enough, so's when he buried the clothes he could have forgotten all about it." Continuing, "Else he was so mind-fogged he'll never really knew it was actually happening."

"Yep, I guess you can't ever take anything for granted."

The men continued to uncover the stash… "Here's our belt with that telltale initial, Boyd!"

"R?"

"Yep."

They found her tennis shoes, but no boots. "I'll bet you a dollar to a donut we can sniff out them boots as we find our way back toward where he first parked and dragged her out for the rape and murder."

"I'll lay out his shirt and pile every piece of clothing in it and tie it up to carry back with us."

As Boyd was busy doing that, Roy was stepping carefully around trying to see where the killer had headed back out toward wherever he staggered off to next.

"Come on, Boyd. I can tell he entered the woods through here-headed back."

Boyd held the bundle close to his chest as he stepped in LeeRoy's foot prints. After half an hour, they figured they had to be within hollerin' distance of the crime scene. No boots yet. Soon, they arrived back at the place Roy had determined the truck had been parked to offload Colleen. "Maybe he didn't get rid of the boots like he did everything else he wore. Maybe he kept them on. Surely, he was freezin' to death by this time, what with stripping off all his clothes."

"Maybe he had an extra set with him in the truck."

"Yeah. Maybe. But somehow, I just don't think drunks usually think like that. All told, I could easily be wrong, too."

"You're right. We know he was out of his head drunk and mad as hell. No way was this premediated. But, I'm grateful we got what we have here. The clothes will give us some idea of the size of our man, and might even have some signs of who they belong to."

"We can hope."

Arriving back at the little cabin, LeeRoy suggested, "Wanna come in and have a bite to eat. It's getting' pretty late and I'm hungry. I know you are."

"Might as well." He grinned, "You fixin' pancakes?"

"If that's what you'd like."

"I'd like!"

"I'll cook a couple pats of sausage and make a pot of coffee. Go on in and head to the bathroom and get cleaned up some. I'll wash up out here by the well house."

Coming back into the kitchen, Boyd said, "Man! I sure do like that soap you got back there. It smells like my Aunt Sophie. That was Mama's sister. We always went to her home during the holidays when I was a boy and she had soap that smelled like that." He shook his head. "Amazing how the smell of something will stir the memories we have stashed in our heads, ain't it?"

"Sure... smells have all sorts of clues imbedded in them. It's a wonder how God provides us with such wonderful things as our senses. Memory and smell are what I call my twin senses." He grinned. "Got me through many a scrape in Vietnam." He was pouring batter onto a round black iron griddle. "Go ahead and fix your coffee."

*

Forensics worked overtime going over each article of clothing worn by the killer. Nothing was found to indicate to whom the clothing belonged, but they were able to conclude they'd belonged to someone who was well over fix feet tall, and weighted around two hundred pounds, give or take a few. The brown hairs they found were those of a Caucasian. The ground-in dirt came from the place where the rape and murder had taken place. If they could just close the gap between the clothes and the owner, then they'd have their man.

All articles were identified, catalogued, and placed in protective bags and boxed; Labeled and stored.

Favored

*

That afternoon in the Trublood trailer office… "Here's the report on the Cotter stand." Bobby placed his findings on the counter and stood the rolled plat to place it back in the container. "Only found a few trees with beetle infestation signs, but nothing to worry about. Getting 'em cut the sooner the better, though. While the weather is cold."

"Thanks, man." Graham perused the report, and smiled. "Looks like your old boss is gonna reap a nice little sum from this timber, Bobby. Good work."

"Mr. Trueblood, I need to take the next few days off if you'll allow it. We've found a place to stay and I need to help get us moved. Ashe can't do it all herself. She's working too."

"Sure, Bobby. Take your time. I won't need another inspection for a while. But I am wanting to take a look-see at a stand of trees that old man Trimnell's been talking of wanting checked out before he makes a decision to cut. But that can wait until you get your family settled in. By the way, where are y'all moving to?"

"Widow Clark's home. She's giving us four nice size rooms upstairs in her house."

"Well! Y'all'll be in high cotton livin' there. That's one more, fine house. In fact, one of the finest in the whole county. Her husband owned more land and industry around these parts than anyone. He had a penchant for turning anything into money. Had his hands in the market too. She ain't sufferin' none for money. He left her well off, I understand."

"We'll be blessed to live there. Ashe will be taking care of the old lady from all I understand. That is, when she's at home-not working at the Country

Club." He stepped toward the door. "I'll probably see you on Monday. Ought to be well done by then."

"Sure, Bobby. See you, bright and early Monday, then."

*

Bobby drove Eddie in to school Friday morning and returned to pick up Ashe at the Marvel Motel. She'd packed everything and together they loaded the car. Bobby hitched the rented truck to the back and they headed out to the Clark mansion. He pulled the car through the car port far enough to where they could easily off load from the trailer and lug the furniture up the stairs.

Jefferson was there, as were four other younger men to help. It seems that Mrs. Clark had enlisted the help of – not only Jefferson, but his four sons as well.

With Ashe directing traffic from the upstairs hall-telling them into which room the items were to be taken, they had completed the offloading in under two hours. After the men left, Ashe said, "Now, the real work begins."

"Tell me what to do and let me at it."

"Head in to the kitchen and fill the sink. Unpack all the kitchen utensils and chinaware. Wash everything, dry them and place them on the table. I'll put them away as soon as I can get our beds made and clothes put away and hung up. When you finish that job, come ask me what's next." She laughed. He smiled.

They took a break at noon and ate a sandwich and drank iced tea. Then Bobby set the alarm clock, he had recently unpacked and placed by his side of their bed, to go off at 2:00. A reminder to go pick up Eddie from school.

*

By the following Monday the apartment was rather well organized. Ashe had even taken the offering of Mrs. Clark and had delved into the attic to borrow a couple of side tables and lamps for use in their living room. She was ecstatic over the outcome of her conversation with Mrs. Clark. And even during the throes of unpacking and placing the furniture, she was able to help her mentor get a wonderful bath. Combing and drying her silver hair they came to know each other very nicely, and declared they would do many more things together.

The days passed quickly and with Easter coming in a few weeks they made plans to attend church together and even dye eggs for the church egg hunt. Ashe was happier than she had been in a long while. She agreed with Adelaide (Mrs. Clark) that a woman needs a woman friend in whom to confide as well as to commiserate. They were going to get along famously.

CHAPTER 18

Day to Day Living

Boyd had called to alert Doctor Hatfield of the evidence gathered and needed his help in finding where Colleen was staying. He needed to take the clothes up to see if she might establish that they belonged to her attacker. Seeing her own shredded clothing might bring back more memories to help in identifying the man.

"Let me contact her Doctor at the Clinic first. Give me a couple of days, Boyd. I'll let you know as soon as I touch base with him that you're coming and when he can expect you."

"You're not even going to trust me with where she's being kept?"

"Of course, you'll be told, but not until you are ready to leave." He smiled, "But I do need to tell you to prepare for at least a five-hour trip each way."

"I appreciate your discretion, Hatfield. Not nearly enough citizens are as astute as yourself in the guarding of dangerous information."

"The fewer people who know, the safer she is. I certainly don't want to be the cause of the killer finding out she's alive and trying to finish the job."

The men shook hands and as Sheriff Boyd turned to leave, "Call me as soon as possible. I'm anxious to be on with this latest evidence."

*

Bobby was sent on inspection tours and upon return, was always greeted fondly by his boss-Graham Trueblood, with words of praise for his expertise in approximating the value of stands of pines throughout the area.

Eddie was doing well in the private school setting too. Learning quickly and enjoying the success of success in his studies.

All was looking bright for the Woodard family as the balmy month of March blew onto the scene.

*

"Wonder where he is?" asked Jolene. "Haven't seen him since he was here raisin' such hell that night a couple weeks back!"

"He's been sent to dry out, Hon. Didn't you know?"

"No, I didn't, but he sure did need it. I hope it works for him. He's a fine man when he's sober. It's a livin' wonder Sheriff Boyd has been able to keep him on the job as long as he has. S'almost like havin' to raise a young'un… dealin' with somebody like him, and expectin' to have him put out."

"Know what you mean," mused Cletus. "I always thought a lot of Junior. Knew his folks from way back when he was just a boy. They were honest, hard workin', people. At least, his mama's people were."

"Aw you're just talkin' to hear yourself. We all know Junior was born with a silver spoon in his mouth! Why his daddy's people were rich enough for five families! Had oil wells somewhere, I think."

"Yeah, but once he got on here in Zacchary, he was regular folks, just like all of us."

They all looked into their coffee cups, (or whatever they were 'into' at the time) and were silent for a few minutes- each with their own thoughts.

Looking up, Colonel asked, "Wonder how Junior got his desire for drink?"

"Don't rightly know, but he had an uncle- Maizie's younger brother, what was a fallin' down drunk." Margie said. "I dated him in high school, and he was drunk most of the time even then. I guess it might run in families or something."

"Drunk in school?" Questioned Jolene.

"Yep. Even though he was able to make class and all, still you could smell it on his breath. Later on, long after I quit with him, you could smell the drink long before he came close." She hesitated, then saw everyone was waiting for something else, "Sure is a sad thing. A fine looking young man, killin' himself little by little and not bein' able to stop."

"I wonder if Junior can win his battle against the bottle?"

Everyone began to stir around, and open up again, "Let's pray so."

"Git that other urn filled and ready. Here comes a new flock of drowsy drivers, girls!" said Cletus.

CHAPTER 19

Guess Who

"You've got a visitor this afternoon, Jane."

"Really? Who is it? Do I know them?" Colleen asked.

"We'll see if you remember him."

"Him? It's a man, then."

"Yes. Doctor Bradley will bring him in, in a few minutes. Here, now. Let's get prettied up some. I'll brush your hair and let you put on a little lipstick. Lipstick always gives a woman the confidence she needs." She smiled and reached into her pockets… handing a small mirror and a tube of 'Crimson Joy' to her patient, she brushed the whimsical blond hair, and tied it back with a wide blue ribbon.

When the two men entered the sunny porch, Colleen was immediately struck with the familiar face of the balding, gray haired man walking toward her with Doctor Bradley. *Now, who is he?* She thought. *I'm sure I must know him.*

He stopped in front of her, and leaned down. "Do you know me, Col - - Jane?"

"I think I'm supposed to, but I don't remember your name. Who are you?"

"I am the sheriff back in a little town down in South Carolina."

"Sheriff? Isn't that a lawman? Are you a lawman?"

"Yes, ma'am. I am. I've come to see if you remember anything about the attack you suffered back in January."

"I've told everything I remember to Betty and she records it on the tape recorder."

"Yes, ma'am. Your Doctor provides me with copies of everything he has about your recollections. And, I must say, you are doing very well in that department. However, now I've brought with me some items of clothing I'd appreciate you taking a look at to see if they are familiar to you in any way. I'm not going to tell you anything about them before you see them… I'm hoping you might be stirred to remember something about them. Are you ready, to take a look?"

"I guess so."

"Betty, let's bring her over here to this table by the window where the light is good." Said Doctor Bradley. "Sheriff, you lay the items out apart, so she can get a good look at each piece."

Jane glanced down at the assorted clothes… a pair of men's dirty jeans, an old belt, a plaid shirt with a torn pocket… *plaid shirt-torn pocket… plaid shirt-torn pocket…* "That's Bobby's shirt!" She blurted out.

"Are you sure?"

"Why, yes. I remember now. He tore that pocket back when we first were married. After I had Eddie… he was just a baby and Eddie grabbed the edge of Bobby's pocket and pulled hard enough to where it tore. Like you see there." She wept silently. Staring back at the clothes, "I finally got enough of seeing them, and so I took all his old clothes that he left at the house after he ran off with Eddie and I put them in a trash bag and threw the whole lot into the dumpster."

"When did you do that?"

"I don't know… a few weeks ago, I guess." She paused a few seconds. "I do know it must have been around Christmas time because I'd taken my little tree down that day. I remember deciding to do some long-put-off cleaning."

"Why'd you wait so long to get rid of his stuff, Jane?"

"I don't know. I guess I just got tired of them taking room in the closet and chest of drawers. Or maybe I was hoping all that time that he'd show back up with my baby." She began to weep.

Boyd reached out and stroked her arm. "I'm so sorry, honey. I didn't come here to get you upset."

"I understand, Sheriff Custer." She beamed. "Sheriff Custer! I know your name! You're our Sheriff back in Zacchary… that's were my home is!"

Doctor Bradley said, "Take Jane back to her room. Dinner will be served in a little while, and she doesn't need more excitement."

"Wait! Please, wait. Might I ask her one more question, Doctor Bradley?"

"Alright, go ahead."

"Do you recall where you discarded the bag of Bobby's clothes?"

"I think it must have been the dumpster out back in the alley between the Police complex and City Hall."

"Why there?"

"It's handy. On my way to or from work. And it's where I always throw my trash." She grinned. "I know now even where I work! THE 95 Truck

Stop!" She was so excited, she began calling out the names of the crew as Betty wheeled her back toward her room.

"Looks like you have your villain, Sheriff."

"Maybe yes, and maybe not," said Boyd. "It just isn't that easy. I wish it was."

CHAPTER 20

Interlude of Little Import

Flora slung her mail truck into the crowded parking area in front of THE 95 Restaurant. She spent a few seconds gathering the flyers and mail for the business as well as the several employees who chose to get their mail there instead of waiting until after work and going home. She entered the door with a flourish of noise and shouted to Jolene, who happened to be nearest the door, "Come git this mail, Hon. I gotta git to the little girl's room."

Taking the bundle of mail from her hands, Jolene took everything back to the break room and laid it all in a pile on the table, and hurried back out front.

When Flora came from around the corner, slinging her hands, she said, "I'm ahead of schedule, so's I'm taking my lunch break early."

"Whatcha want, Hon?"

"Has Cletus made any hash lately?"

"Sure. He's always got hash on the weekend. You want a bait of hash and rice?"

"Yeah. And some iced tea and a sweet pickle or two."

"Be right up. I'll pour your tea as soon as I put this in."

As Margie was hanging the written order by a plastic clothes pin to the wire across the window to the kitchen, Flora was talking to her back and to anyone else in hearing distance. "You know... somebody needs to send somebody out to the old Blackburn place."

"Why?" asked Margie as she poured the iced tea into a clear plastic glass and laid a paper-wrapped straw and a napkin roll of silverware in front of her customer.

"Them new people... well, they ain't all that new-been living out there about four months now. Well, anyway, they... and I'm speakin' of the daddy now, he's mean as a rattlesnake! I never seen his wife, but his little children-three of 'em, play outside in the worst weather with practically no clothes on at all. And the dogs are starvin' to death!

"Oh my God. Someone ought to call Social Services and the animal people on him." Margie stood silently, the said, "Why don't you call them."

"Simply because I know I'll be the first one he'll suspect has done it and to tell the truth, he looks dangerous to me. His wife never comes outside. At least not when I'm coming by. But the little babies... three of them, I think. Probably two, three, and maybe four, are always outside with barely anything on. They play under the trailer to get out of the weather. I swear before God they need to be taken from their parents."

"You know what you need to do?" Answering her own question, Margie said, "Tell Sheriff Custer! He'll go out there and call whoever needs to be called on them people."

She reached and placed the plate of hash, rice, half dozen slices of sweet pickle, and two warm rolls in front of Flora. "Enjoy."

"Just what I need to get me on around the route and end out my week."

*

LeeRoy had hidden his truck half a mile back from his target. The hour was just after five in the morning, so he needed to not waste any time, if he wanted to situate himself so he could observe unseen as the sun rose and exposed his surroundings.

He moved silently through the thick woods and underbrush heading toward what had once been the old abandoned singlewide on Jeb Blackburn's land. He'd heard that Jeb had let it out to some out-of-towners somewhile back. He'd soon find out if what was reported about that was fact or fiction.

He had evidently gotten close enough for the dogs to smell his presence and could hear the two barking in the near distance from the yard. He felt for the chunks of meat he'd brought in case he'd need it. Nearing the trailer, he could make out the outline of it in the darkness.

About that time the door slammed open and Roy could make out a large man stalking toward the cowering dogs. Roy wept as he heard the man threaten to beat the dogs to death! They whined and finally quieted. "Shut up! Shut up! I'll kill you right now and get us all out of our misery!" He stomped back into the trailer and slammed the door.

Roy had a maddening urge to attack and kill the man then and there. *Oh, God. Please help the woman and children. Take care of them, please. Amen.*

A light was turned on in the back. Roy assumed it was the bathroom as the window was small. In just a few seconds, it was doused, and all was silent.

He lay still and waited for daylight. He wasn't leaving until he was satisfied that he knew everything he could about this situation to relate to Sheriff Custer. It was by his directive that LeeRoy was on this mission.

Roy stayed as still as possible in order to contain his odor so the dogs would not be aroused again. He gently swept leaves over himself and lay propped on a low stump and dozed on and off.

Pretty soon there began a gently perceptible hint of light in the east. With eyes already adjusted to the dark, his vision was really keen. At this juncture, he could see a rusty swing set in the side yard, beyond which was a clothes line with a couple of, what looked like, towels hanging limply… maybe it was diapers… the emaciated dogs curled together beneath a bush. A beat-up pickup was parked perpendicular to the house trailer and was facing out the short drive toward the rocky road. Back nearer to where he lay, was a four-wheeled, high-sided wooden hauling trailer. Roy could easily detect the odor of manure emanating from the floor of it. *He must be using this to haul cattle. Wonder if this is who's been rustlin' folk's cattle from around here?*

The little-used road was narrow, and here where it dipped low, the place was nothing but smooth rocks. In wet weather the road became flooded and water flowed across the road almost knee deep. Otherwise it was easily passable, although seldom used by any traffic except for the mailman and maybe a hunter or two during deer and turkey seasons. The trailer was the only dwelling on Hangman's Creek Road, which derived its' name from a huge oak that grew close to the creek, where too many innocent lives were snuffed out by lies told and attested to by those who held grudges… or simply wanted to see a man hanged.

At seven, a light came on in the rear end of the trailer. Within a few minutes another lit up the front end. Roy supposed they were up making breakfast. He listened for the sound of children, but heard nothing. Not even the sounds of activity. Five minutes later the lights were out. Roy watched as the door was swung open and the big man stepped out and peed in the yard, then headed to the truck. He drove out and up the road away from town... toward a frontage road to 26.

LeeRoy stayed where he was for another hour. The lights came on again and he could discern the sounds of children and the wife getting dressed and making breakfast. His mouth watered when he smelled sausage frying. Pretty soon, he saw a small boy come out with a shallow pan with scraps for the dogs. They devoured the food before the child even got turned back around to head back into his house. *Those dogs need water. They need to be taken away just like the babies do. God help 'em. I wonder if the wife is in as bad a shape as the dogs are.*

He was soon rewarded with the sight of the woman and the children. He saw only two children. Boyd had told him there were three. It was light enough for them to see and be seen. There was a small dark suitcase carried in her left hand and the two children at her right holding hands. She was a slight woman, dressed in a too-large dress beneath a hip-length heavy sweater. It appeared she was wearing overlarge shoes and long socks. The children wore pants and jackets and caps pulled over their ears. He estimated the children to be somewhere between two and four years old. With the way they were dressed he could not tell whether they were boys or girls or one of each. He also was unable to see if they were too thin or bruised. None of the trio was limping. She had them moving at a fairly good clip. The children had to run to keep up with their mother.

Moving from his position, he followed them as they turned out of the yard and headed in the opposite direction from that taken by the man. They walked nearly a mile before she stopped and pulled the children off the road into a stand of young pines. She was able to keep the children quiet. He supposed they were used to being told to 'shut up'.

Several times traffic went by. Probably folks on their way to work. A school bus came by loaded with children. But thirty minutes after the woman had hidden herself and the children, a dark blue sedan drove by, slowed down, but sped back up. He watched as it turned around at the next road and came slowly back. He was rewarded to watch the woman and the children step out of their hiding place and run toward the car. A door was opened, and they got in. No time was wasted. The vehicle pulled back out into the road and sped off. LeeRoy memorized the Georgia tag number.

*

"We got 'em both!" cried Boyd. "The pickup belongs to a Slade Mellencamp, and the blue Chevy is registered to Ansel Triplin. It appears that Mister Triplin is a lawyer from Atlanta."

LeeRoy grinned and poured two cups of fresh hot coffee. They were seated at the little table in the darkened cabin two days after his last missiom.

"You done hit the jackpot for us, LeeRoy!" Smiling he took a gulp of the hot coffee and he continued, "Lawyer Triplin was able to keep Slade outa prison. It was about four years ago. Seems they made a deal someway to trade information for time. Slade turned in his buddies that were dealers here in South Carolina. They were able to get some real big suckers trafficking drugs up out of Florida and running them all up the East Coast."

"Why on earth did his wife meet Triplin the other morning?"

"Your guess is as good as mine. All's I can say is the tag's registered to him. Anybody coulda' been driving it, though"

"How is she? And the children?"

"Don't rightly know. But, she's more than likely with relatives somewhere safe, I'd say." He stood, "I got the humane folks to go down there and see to th' dogs. I understand they weren't in too rough 'a shape. Teddy told me they'd give 'em their shots and worm 'em and have 'em ready to adopt soon. Said they were real good huntin' hounds somebody is sure to want to pick up for a song."

"Well, good. But what about him? He hasn't been home since the other morning when I saw him leave?"

"Nope. We think he's hooked up again with another supplier. Hasn't been seen since he left. But LeeRoy, I gotta' tell you I have a mightly sneaky feelin' they've got him sniffin' for the drug traffic again. I think that's why his lawyer took the wife and kids. But, not to worry. We can find him if we decide he might be our killer. Never fear… we can find him."

"Well, you can strike him off your list of suspects. I can promise you there's no way he's your killer. Nothing about him would fit any of the evidence so far. He's not the right size, nor is the vehicle right. You can rest assured, Sheriff, he ain't the one you want for Colleen's murder. Maybe for something else, but not for that."

Boyd slapped LeRoy's shoulder. "Thanks. Now get some rest. I'll be back in touch soon. And thanks for the coffee. Your's is always the best."

CHAPTER 21

Hope House Complex

Cuthbert Woolsley's, was the first friendly face Junior came upon when he entered the door of Hope House. The man was mopping the tile floor of the great room. Junior took in his surroundings in a few seconds of concentrated effort. *Four green plastic covered couches. A couple stacks of some six or so, plastic chairs in the corner. One very large-screened TV over a case holding a DVD player. A tall, wide shelved case full of hardback, as well as paperback books. A bunch of DVD's too. Bet they're mostly porn.* He mentally snorted, then amended his conjecture about the DVD's. *Probably religious!*

He grinned at the mopper, and stopped to put out his hand. "I'm William T. Raeford, but you can call me Junior."

Taking the proffered hand, the shiny-faced black man said, "Pleased to meet you. My name is Cuthbert Woolsley, but you can call me Wooly, if it pleases you."

Pumping hands the two men sized each other up. Junior surmised the slight man could hold his own in any altercation. *Wiry more'n Wooly. Arms like lightered knots. Shaved head. Black beady eyes over an unusually thin nose. English blood somewhere back there.*

'Pears to be a fair-minded sort. Big man-used to being obeyed or listened to... maybe a man of some distinction. Pity he ended up here. Maybe he's an 'Undercover' for Travis, thought Wooly.

"I'm here to check myself in, Wooly. Where's the Boss man?"

Turning to point toward the first door into a shallow hallway, "In there."

"Is it a Mister Peters?"

"That's him, alright, Mister Maxwell Peters to be exact." And Wooly returned to his mopping, as Junior stepped toward the open door.

Peering inside he found the sparsely furnished room empty. Looking back at Wooly, he asked, "Any further guess as to where he might be?"

Turning to point toward the wide, open hall toward the rear of the building, "Might be in the kitchen. You can't miss it... just follow the smells." And he grinned, showing glistening white teeth.

Junior sauntered down the short hall and found himself staring into a huge dining room, beyond which was a large, open kitchen. There were half a dozen men in white aprons milling around the pristine area as if they knew what they were doing. The odor was tantalizing. Reminded Junior of THE 95, and the smells emanating from Cletus' kitchen.

A tall, thin black man looked around from where he'd stationed himself inspecting the serving line. Smiling and walking toward Junior, he spoke. "My good man. Welcome! Am I addressing a Mister Raeford?"

"Why, yes. You evidently were expecting me?"

"Indeed. Your Sheriff Custer apprised us of your imminent arrival, sir. We are happy to have you with us, and pray your stay will prove to be very successful and even enjoyable for the most part." He smiled a wide-open-unassuming grin. "Come, I'll get you oriented to your surroundings, and show you to your quarters." He paused momentarily, and said, extending his hand, "I am Maxwell Peters. Director of Hope House and ever at your service."

Junior followed the man back into the great room and stood where he was… watched as Peters closed the gap between himself and Wooly. Peters leaned in, and spoke too softly for Junior to hear a word spoken. He soon saw Wooly peering at him over Peters' shoulder, and was relieved to see him nodding back at 'the boss'. Peters then turned and motioned for Junior to follow him down the wide hall, past the office and on into a two-story dormitory. Stairs rose off to the left as well as the right side, but they moved on past the stairs. Every twenty feet or so they passed an open door. Junior was able to quickly glance inside to view barracks-style cots… appeared to be two to a room… a long table with two metal chairs and he thought there might be an area to lounge, but wasn't sure if that was a single soft chair or maybe a couch. *Oh well, guess I'll soon find out.*

"Here." Stopping by the last room on the right of the hall-just before a closed exit door at the very end, 'Boss' said, "You'll be calling this your home for the time being. I hope you'll find it up to your standards of privacy and comfort, Mister Raeford. And just so you know we're open, and above board with every patron here… your assigned brother's room is located directly across from yours. He will become very aware of you during your time with us… that is, at the beginning. Until you get your bearings."

"Who's going to be my brother?" Asked Junior.

"Mister Woolsley."

Junior nodded in understanding. Then, he entered the space and was very surprised to find only one bed, a soft chair next to a table holding a metal-based lamp of generous proportions. Near the window was a neat desk, with small lamp and a desk chair with low arms. A bookcase-half empty- was standing in the corner on an angle with a small-leaved tree in a pot behind it. It looked real to Junior. The walls were painted a very pleasant cream color and the spread and drapes were of a deep-colored western design. The bedside rug was an earth tone which showed nicely against the dark concrete floors. Over his bed hung the portrait of some fresh-faced cavalry officer. *Must be somebody special.* Along the other walls were several nice pictures of Southwestern Indians with pottery of various designs. Overall, the room was more than comfortable. *Hope that cot is easy to get used to.*

Peters crossed the room in a few quick steps and drew open the drapes to expose a large window... barred, but, giving an expansive view of a large farm beyond. Silo, sheds, barn, tractors, and horses held in a large corral. He became aware of a much larger pasture over to the right-this side of a heavily wooded area. There were half-a-dozen black and white dairy cows grazing there.

"This sure is pretty country. Does this farm go with this facility?"

"Indeed, it does, Mister Raeford. This is how most of our patrons are fed- by our own labors." He pulled the drapes back across the window. "Come back to the office and I'll bring you up to date on everything that's expected of you."

"Mister Peters, might I ask as to why there are bars on the window?"

"Certainly. This facility was originally built as an asylum for those with deep mental issues. They could not assimilate into the society at that time. Since those days, however, great strides have been made and with the proper medications, most people suffering from mental issues are able to take their places in our society. This place became derelict and I found it for a song... so to speak." He continued to walk toward the door. "I hope you can approve of the aura surrounding this edifice. A great many strides and changes have taken place since we've been here."

"How long has it been?"

"Almost twenty years. We are making upgrades nearly constantly. And, by the way, during your sojourn with us, if you see something that you believe would elevate our surroundings even further, please, never hesitate to bring it to my attention. In fact, most of the improvements done were accomplished from suggestions brought by our patrons."

"Well, it's certainly more than I expected. When I heard I was being given the "opportunity to avail myself of your service" (he used both hands to place quotations around that last phrase), I confess, I did not want to come. But I have changed my mind. I'm anxious to 'get to work' on my behavior with the proper help."

"Come, let's head to my office."

"I hate to throw a snag into your orientation, Mister Peters, but I need to use the nearest john."

Jumping somewhat, Peters quickly led his charge back into the hall way. Stopping in front of a door next to the room they'd just vacated, he said, "In here, Sir. Between every other room is a bathroom. You are free to use any vacant one you come to. However, you must leave it pristine, as it will contain the toiletries of the men next door. As yours shall." Opening the door, he showed Junior the nondescript letters of WC printed at eyelevel. "I'll wait for you in the office. You know where it is, I believe."

"Forgive my ignorance, Sir. What does the WC stand for?"

Smiling broadly, "It's borrowed from the European usage for 'Water Closet'. Old term for commode, or 'john'… in our terms… I just thought I might instill a bit of wisdom as well as humor into such a mundane commodity."

"Yes sir." Shaking his head, Junior realized he'd better get prepared for getting back home with a whole lot more education than he left with. Smiling, he entered the white-tiled room.

Favored

*

After having been provided with his 'uniform', toiletries, inside slippers, two sets of bed sheets, two towels and wash clothes. Peters impressed upon Junior that at all times each man was expected to greet and speak with others in modulated voice, as well as with the utmost respect. No accounting for age, or color. The list of "EXPECTATIONS" was handed to Junior with: "You'll want to read, reread, and memorize this outline of your daily duties. You're given a leeway of around fifteen minutes of noncompliance unless you've been given a green slip of 'FREE TIME' by myself or by a Trustee. That trustee can be changed as often as once a month. You'll find him always wearing a small silver star on his shirt collar during his hours of duty. Too, you'll know his identity by their photograph on the bulletin board in the front room, as well as the one in the mess hall. One of those two areas will be visited by you every day for your orders, for that particular day, week, or month… according to your progress. You, Mister Raeford, will find your orders, for the time being, under the *RED BANNER* section. Pay no attention to the orders given beneath the other banners as they will not apply to you. As you progress you'll be expected to accomplish more and different tasks. The appropriate clothing will be provided at such time… according to the duty assigned then."

"Boy, y'all sure got some big operation here." Junior smiled. "We oughta incorporate some of these ideas into our penal system." By now, Junior was grinning… *This is gonna be a piece of cake,* he thought.

Sitting forward in his desk chair, Mister Peters spoke. "Get to your quarters and sort out your belongings, and get your bed made." Rising, he started for the door, "I'll see you in mess within fifteen minutes." Glancing at his watch. "Don't be late."

Junior felt like saluting, but contained his ardor. "Yessir."

*

After quickly stripping away the spread, he made the bed with sheets that he assumed were for his room alone. They were a deep maroon color which matched the dark colors of the print in the drapes and of the spread. He then changed into the blue trousers and shirt, sandals (keeping his socks on), he hung his city clothes in the tiny closet and headed to the WC where he washed his face and hands. Then he headed on down the way toward the mess hall. Well before he turned the corner from the large area known as the common room, he could hear the noises of many voices and the clatter of dishes and utensils. He entered the double doors to the sounds of odors of the 'mess hall'. His entrance barely made a ripple in the tide of men flowing past him in a slow-moving line toward the far end of the room. As he sought the end of the line, an arm reached out and drew him into a 'held back' space. "Greetings, friend. I'm Taylor Simpson. You're new ain't- aren't you?"

Glancing at the small, ball-headed patron, Junior said, "Yes. Sir. I am new. He put out his hand to shake and continued, "I just got here this morning."

"Well, I'll be praying for you to get along well, and to thank God for this opportunity you're being given. If you can't recover in this place, friend, you must be in the worst shape of anyone I ever heerd-heard of." He smiled.

"Where were all these men earlier? I've been here a couple of hours, and never saw another soul except Mister Woolsey and Boss."

"Don't call him 'Boss', Sir. Didn't he tell you that we should not use nicknames? He's Director Peters except when he in the pulpit on Sundays, then he's Reverend Peters."

"Yes. I forgot. I think I did see that on my sheet of 'EXPECTATIONS'." Thinking of 'Wooly', he asked, "Then, why did Wooly ask me to call him by his nickname?"

"Oh, that's because he, that is, Wooly, told you to call him that. Ya see… using a 'good' nickname is Okay, but it's when you feel like callin' somebody a bad name… well, that's when it ain't – uh, isn't allowed."

He grinned at his new companion, and as they continued to shuffle ever nearer to the food line, he asked, "Do you suppose I'll ever learn all of those expectations? I'm afraid I'll ever be messin' up."

"Awh… you'll learn them soon enough. It's kinda' like going back to school. We have instructions in proper English two times a week, in the evenings. We meet here in the hall after supper on Tuesdays and Thursdays for a couple hours, I guess. Anyway, I'm grateful for it. I was raised by a pair of wolves, I think!" He grinned. "You'll soon see. This is way better than any other place we could have found ourselves. I think Director Peters is really tryin' to git us all to speak better and leave our past really in the past."

Junior turned and picked up a large aluminum tray and a bundle of heavy stainless utensils wrapped in a cloth napkin. *A cloth napkin! Wow. Guess we do laundry too?* "Do we do our own laundry?"

"That's right. We're taught everything. And, here we learn how to be frugal…" He grinned again. "Now, that was a new word for me, Mister Raeford. Frugal. And I do think every living soul needs to learn it and what it means."

Junior passed his tray to the first server and smiled. "Do I get a choice of what or how much?" He asked the man.

"Afraid not, friend. But I'm telling you this meal will provide everything your body needs in the way of nutrients and for repairing damage that may be done to one who has misused himself. Be sure to eat it all. Best food you'll ever have eaten, to my way of thinking. You won't suffer from hunger here." He smiled and slid the tray on up the line for the next server to place more food in the sections. Ending at the desserts, Junior saw they were all apple pie wedges. Good thing he loved apple pie. He was given the choice of either iced tea or water to drink. He took the tea and prayed it was good and sweet.

Seated at a long table between two friendly faces, he spoke to the new acquaintance. "Mister Taylor Simpson, how long have you been here, if I might ask?"

"Sure. You can ask. Ask anyone anything you want to. I've been here going on four months, and if I had my druthers, I'd stay here. But, pity is I cannot. My space is needed. I'm nearly ready to graduate back into that evil old world. I get scared just thinking about it."

Junior was halfway through his delicious lunch when Mister Peters stopped by. A hand was placed upon his shoulder, and Peters leaned over to say, "Come to my office after your meal. Do not rush, though."

He nodded and said, "Yessir." Turning to Taylor... "Umgh... Wonder what this's about?" He asked, looking askance at this newest friend.

"Oh. Protocol, is all."

"Protocol? What's protocol?"

"Kinda a proven way of doing things... kinda like upholding the law, maybe."

"Do'ya suppose I've messed up already?" Asked Junior.

"Hardly!" Taylor laughed, shaking his head. "No. This is par for the course with newcomers. He'll probably want to get some real close information from you." He took another big forkful of chicken salad from the shredded lettuce nest. "You give him everything. Do what you can do to let him have the best idea of your life and problems now."

"Kinda scared… Like you about getting out and me comin' in, I guess."

"I understand, friend, but be assured that you have nothing to fear from this place. Hope House is known all over the United States as the place producing the most positive results with those of us blessed enough to come here."

"If you say so."

"At assembly this evening, sit with me and let me know how it went with your indoctrination."

Junior nodded and dug into the apple pie.

*

Within a couple of days, Junior had learned the ropes enough to become relaxed in body, if not in mind. He continually thought about how the smell and taste of alcohol was so pleasant. He often salivated onto his pillowcase at night when he dreamed the vivid dreams of lifting the bottle to his lips and gulping down the burning-satisfying liquid. He cried often, not from sorrow, but for himself, and his desire to overcome, yet so deeply fearful of failing. He did not want to fail again. *God help me!* He thought.

CHAPTER 22

Another Clue

The facility was quiet. Darkness bathed the hallways… interdicted by small lamps at the nurse's stations. Too, every thirty feet or so were small floor lights to aid in the foot traffic that was always prevalent in such settings. Colleen slept deeply as did her companion who was bedded down in the comfortable suede recliner not two feet from the hospital bed. The hour was nearly three. In a short while the shifts would be changing.

Betty awoke to something and glanced at her large-faced watch. She stood and reached out to see if Colleen was cold… had mussed the covers someway. *God! She appears to be catatonic! Eyes wide open and a dead expression on her face.* Just before Betty pressed the buzzer for help, Colleen turned her face and stared at Betty.

"I know who it was!" Tears began to stream from her eyes.

Betty turned on the small lamp where it would not invade their eyes. She leaned over the patient. "Oh my God! You know?"

"Yes. Get the recorder."

In less than thirty seconds Betty had the lights turned up and the recorder ready. "It is 2:55 the morning of March eighteenth, 1999. Colleen Woodard will speak."

She sat back down as Colleen situated herself higher into the bed. Blowing her nose, she glanced out the black window and spoke: "The night I suffered that horrendous attack, I now recall catching a glimpse of the man's hand as he was dragging me by my arm through the dark woods. I definitely remember seeing a heavy gold chain bracelet on his wrist." She broke and began to sob, but kept on, even through her hiccups. "I know we all heard that Junior's daddy sent it to him from overseas somewhere when he graduated college. I never saw another bracelet quite like it before or since." She fell back upon the pillow.

"Anything else you need to say?"

"Not now, Betty. I'm dying from knowing this! How could he change into such a monster? We've been friends for ages. All our lives, almost. It's just unbelievable! Surely to God there's an explanation. Maybe he was high on some bad drug, or something." She snubbed and blew her nose. "We all knew he and my Bobby drank, but they never turned mean." She looked over at Betty. "At least, not that I ever knew."

"Try to see if you can get back to sleep. You seem to be coming around so well, now. I don't think depriving yourself of sleep's gonna help you to heal. You can tell Doctor Bradley in the morning." Betty was helping Colleen to get resettled into the covers. "Need to go to the bathroom? Need a sleeping aid?"

"No. I think I'll be alright… just never would have believed this… I'll just lie here and talk to God for a while. He'll calm my soul." Looking up toward the dim lights behind her bed she said, "Douse the lights, Betty."

CHAPTER 23

Finders Keepers

Chester awoke from his cardboard mansion earlier than usual. The traffic along 'his stretch of 95' had hardly wavered in its' intensity throughout the cool night. Mostly the big rigs rumbled their lullaby during the darkest hours… tires singing their love songs to the pavement… leaving imperceptible vestiges of themselves along the way. Chester was in love too. He loved his life, his comfortable place, his friends, but mostly he was enamored of his freedom. Nobody to tax his brain with commands. Lord knew, he'd had enough of that during his stint in service to his country. With his disappearance from the rolls of the military, he was soon declared to be deceased and someone else pocketed his portion of retirement. *Some bureaucrat probably. I don't need it nor want it,* he declared to himself… on many occasion. Still, there were times he suddenly felt the urgent need for money-more than his gleanings from along the intersection over his head. Thus far, he was able to work his mind through those desires, and soon was content again with life. But! Coming across that chunky gold bracelet gave him pause for wondering exactly what he was going to do with it. *Finders, keepers!* He'd heard that all his life. But this time… with something this expensive, maybe there is a reward out for its' return. He'd sure feel better about it than trying to hock it somewhere. Paulie at the pawn would surely want to know how he came about having it! What would he tell him? That he just found it on the side of the road? Which he actually had. Paulie would want to know where and when. Sheriff Boyd would be called… *Oh hell! I might's as well take it on in to old Boyd and turn it over. I can't fool myself into trying to keep this thing for myself. After all, I'm too content with my life. Don't want no interceptions nor interruptions!* He reasoned.

Sitting at the bar, he gave his order to Selma. "The usual, Hon."

Winking, she said, "Right. Coming up. Hon!"

Won't hurt if I mebbe show the bracelet to my family here. They can give me some advice on what to do with it.

As The plate of breakfast foods was placed on the bar in front of him, Colonel put his coffee cup down onto the folded napkin and reached inside his shirt pocket. With no fanfare, he laid the heavy, gold bracelet along the dark marble behind his plate. "What's you think of this, Selma?"

"Gawd! Colonel! Who in the world give you that?" She reached to pick it up.

"No! Don't touch it. I don't want nobody bothering it."

She looked at him, "Why? You think I'd try to take it from you?" Turning she stomped back toward the urn, and then looked back… "'S probably fake anyway."

"No Siree. Ain't nothin' fake about this 'un. I can tell this is at least 18 karats… maybe more. I'll wager this thing'll weigh five or six ounces. Bring a pretty penny. I just don't know if I want to sell it. I'll never get what it's worth."

He lowered his head and began to scarff down the hot grits and scrambled eggs.

"Well, good mornin' y'all!" Called Margie. "How's everybody this fine morning?"

"You mighty bright eyed and bushy tailed this morning! Got a little from 'Who's 'is Face' last night did'cha?"

"Oh! Shut up Selma. You an' Milford ain't been at it since last Christmas!"

The air erupted with glee. Remembering how, at the party Milford was looped enough to confess how Selma had given him a 'bump and grind' the night before. The group each had their own mental images of the owner of THE 95 and wife going at it.

Laughter was raucous and hearty for a few minutes until Margie staggered-cross legged- (everybody knew what that meant) as those behind the counter moved aside so she could scurry toward the back. As she moved down the bar she stopped stock still as her eyes fell upon the gold bracelet. Suddenly- with all thoughts of the restroom on hold, she asked, "Where'd you find Junior's bracelet?"

As one voice, they asked, "Junior's bracelet?"

"Yes. That is Junior's bracelet. Got word from Boyd to be on the lookout for it." And with that she sped off toward the back.

"Gosh! Y'all, I didn't have no idea this thing was Junior's."

The group all stared at it. Each wondering exactly when it was lost and where it was found. Knowing that he'd surely want it back. But he was away for a while longer up at Hope House.

Speaking all at once, they bombarded Colonel with suggestions. After a few seconds, he spoke through and said, "I'm taking it in to Boyd. Soon's I finish up here. He'll know. It'll be kept safe 'til Junior gets back."

Nodding and agreeing they all turned to their duties as Margie came back into the area. "Y'all all look mighty smug. What'd y'all talk about behind my back."

"Aw, Margie. Don't let your imagination go running off. We just decided what Colonel's doing with the bracelet."

"Yeah. An' wha's that?"

"Naw, Margie. They didn't decide nuthin'. I decided by myself. I'm taking it to Boyd for safekeeping, 'til Junior gets out."

"Um humh." She kept her head down. "Y'all do know that it's been told… (she lowered her head and glanced to her right and then to her left in a surreptitious way) …that Boyd is Junior's real daddy."

As one the listeners raised up and gasped, wide-eyed. "What?" They all looked around at each other to see if anyone else knew of this rumor. "Naw. Never heard that!"

"Yep. Years ago, it was. Boyd and Juniors mother were in love, but for some reason she was pressured into a marriage to Billy Raeford. Somebody said something about her daddy had some dirt on the Custer family and swore he'd have Boyd killed if his baby daughter married him. So… it seems she was forced to marry the Raeford boy. They say that the night before the wedding she slipped out and met Boyd and Junior was the result." She stood back and let the story sink in. "Now that story's been shelved all these years, but Junior's mama and daddy had a good marriage from everything anybody knows."

Busy with replenishing the stack of paper cups… she continued. "But Junior was the only child they had. Seems no body was concerned about Junior bein' their only child… said it was a fluke of nature when Billy's daddy told about when he had mumps and they 'fell', when he was a football star in college. Makes the supposition of Junior being Boyd's even more credible, don't it?"

"Yes. The elder is the Reverend Richard Barnard. Ever at work for His Lord in our penal systems throughout the world. You've heard of him, surely."

"Oh, yes. He's quite well known to all of us who work in law enforcement capacities. But, I had no idea this place existed, nor that it was so closely connected to Richard. But I cannot fathom why I've never heard of The Barnard Clinic."

"As Director I only have so many spaces for the proper attention to be given to those I alone deem would benefit most from this facility. Consequently, we do not advertise our existence, but rely upon word of mouth to gateway the women into treatment here."

"No men?"

"No, afraid not. We determined long ages back that there are entirely too many women traumatized by men to even consider treating them here as well. This exclusiveness takes a lot of stress off our patients as well as the staff."

"I understand the need for that. Well, it's one lovely place. Thank you, Doctor Bradley for being so gracious with addressing my nosiness." She smiled, "Now… I've been speaking with Colleen concerning the trauma she's come through and need to know if you have any reasonable thought as to when she might be able to leave this facility." She continued, "Possibly long enough for us to fulfil her wish to face her attacker in person."

"Ummmm. Let me consider this first in order that I might get to the conclusion she desires." He looked at Betty. "Would you please bring her latest report to me, Dear?"

Betty left the room without a word.

"Now, tell me all about what you're expecting to do, or accomplish on the suggested foray."

For the next several minutes Colleen did most of the talking. Explaining why she felt compelled to see Junior face to face. Her arguments were very valid, and Doctor Bradley was in tune with her need to see this through. He knew she was strong enough physically, but his only concern dealt with her mental strength. He vacillated between her tenderness and possible loss of her present hold on reality, and her eventual need to face the demons of her past in order to slay them and be victorious for her future.

Betty handed him the thin file, and he sat back, opened it and the room was silent… every eye upon him as he read. They each watched his countenance to see if they might glean something of his thoughts… only to be disappointed. Doctor Bradley was a master of his emotions. Knowing everyone was watching he'd smile every so often, just to throw his guests off guard. With a mischievous laugh out-loud, he enjoyed watching everyone ease back into their chairs. "I see no reason to preclude Colleen from taking that trip. With the proper preparation, she can be made comfortable in an ambulance for the long trip, if necessary. I can also alert Hatfield to have a room ready for her to stay the night there in Zacchary. But, she must return here as quickly as is feasible after the meeting. And, she must have every protection during the meeting." He rose, as did Boyd, and said, "In fact, I'd appreciate having a taping of the entire exchange between those two for my records." Turning back, he said, "It is a pleasure to meet you all, and now, Betty… do the details of preparing Colleen for her trip. Have everything in place for the hour of her departure that Sheriff Boyd tells you."

Before long, Colleen began to weep again. "I know I cannot stop crying, but I feel so grateful that my Doctor knows I'm strong enough to make the trip. I can barely wait to face Junior. There's so much I need to say to him."

Amanda moved near and reached over to slip her arm around the shoulders of the lovely young woman, "You're stronger than you've ever been in your life before. You've come through this… you can go through anything and walk out on the far side better equipped and happier than you would ever have considered prior to those awful events. Wait and see."

"Thank you, Amanda. Might I call you Amanda?"

"Wouldn't have it any other way, Colleen, dearest."

*

Late that evening-back in Zacchary, at THE 95 they ordered the big hamburger plate, piled with French fries specially cut in the kitchen, along with the hottest, freshest coffee this side of the Atlantic.

"You callin' Hope House tomorrow?"

"Don't think I'll wait 'til tomorrow. Think I'll give Maxwell a 'see-to' tonight. He's always available, and it won't be too late when we get outa here. I'd like him to begin the process of getting Junior prepared. I want to see this through as fast as possible. This crime is about to kill me… knowing all we do about these two great kids."

She nodded and continued chewing and licking her fingers. "Kinda anxious myself. I know I'd love to see a positive closure to this mess." She swallowed, "You do know it's possible, don't you… a positive end?"

"Yeah? How?"

"Well, I don't know exactly, but things might just work out where both of them are 'healed'- if you get my drift."

"Boy, I sure need to pray that can happen. Nothing could make me happier than to see both of these kids on the best side of mending. Even if Junior spends heavy time in prison… he can still come out on top of this mess. Don't you think?"

"Sure. We'll just need to keep a positive attitude and go with the flow and let the two of them work it out. Maybe I'd better include the baby as well, and young Eddie too."

"Can't leave them out. I think they'd be the most important ones in this whole mess when you come right down to it."

*

Driving off in the quietly purring vehicle, Amanda waved from her open window, "See you first thing tomorrow."

Boyd waved back and entered the building and straight back to his office. Lifting the receiver, he dialed Hope House.

"Did I catch you at a bad time?"

"No... is this Boyd?"

"Unh huh. Just got in from talking with Colleen Woodard. You know, our victim. Well, she's doing real good and has come to the conclusion she wants to see Junior when you feel it can be arranged. What d'you think?"

"Yes? Well. let me see." Silence. "Can I call you tomorrow? I need to observe Junior a little longer. I don't know if he's up to it just yet. He's still jumpy even though he's on something to help him through this. I'll give you a call just as soon as I deem he might be ready enough to face her. That okay?"

"It'll have to be. You just keep this on the front burner and give me a heads-up as soon as you think he's ready."

"Count on it."

"Thanks." And Boyd hung up his phone. Somewhat disappointed that Max felt Junior wasn't yet up to the meeting, he admonished himself for being so antsy about his feelings. He knew better than try to rush things ... could collapse the house of cards which was already trembling. He smiled at the pictures in his head.

"Headin' out, Tony. Keep on top. Call me if you need to."

"G'night Boss."

CHAPTER 29

Junior's Miracle

"What do you mean… talk to me? You gotta be kiddin' Mister Peters. I cannot imagine she'd ever want to see my ugly face again after what I did!"

"Be that as it may, Mister Raeford, it's evident to me that this is something she needs to do. You may or may not feel up to this meeting for the present time, but I'd suggest you spend a good deal of time in prayer and self-reflection concerning what you might deem to be best for her, and not for yourself."

"So, you're telling me it's ultimately up to me as to whether or not this meeting would take place? I've got the trump card?"

"That's about it. She cannot force you, nor can I. But, I do want you to think and pray. Tonight, after our regular discussions in assembly, I'd ask that you sequester yourself in your room, slip the 'do not disturb' sign on your door, and just play within your mind the mental pictures that might arise from such a meeting. Try to hear what you might think she'd tell you… think of your replies and thoughts. That's the most efficient and fruitful avenue to take to help you decide to actually see your friend face to face. Certainly, if she-the victim, wants to face you, then you need to do all in your power to aid in her healing from the trauma that you brought about, don't you think?"

"Okay. I'll do as you suggest. Just let me get through the discussions. I know all the men are waitin' to hear what I need to tell them tonight."

"You'll do fine, Mister Raeford. It's easy for me to see that you're facing your demons with great security and strength… getting stronger in mind as well as body. You're doing well, never doubt it." Max rose, "I'll see you after dinner in assembly."

*

Junior realized that earlier, in the assembly, he had not said nearly everything that he'd thought he needed to. He left with a sense of incompleteness bugging him and he was unable to pinpoint exactly what. Later, in the dark, Junior spent so long on his knees until when he tried to get up… after his final 'amen', that he had some difficulty, consequently, he simply crawled over to his chair and lifted himself up into it… pulled on the lamp light of his desk. Immediately, his eyes swept to his Bible. He reached and picked it up, absently flipping through the pages. He laid it down and with his right hand pushed from right to left, letting the pages fold away in chunks. Finally, he stopped and there before him he saw the words leap off the page. He read them out loud; _Then Job answered the Lord, and said, I know that thou canst do everything, and that no thought can be withholden from thee. Who is he that hideth counsel without knowledge? Therefore have I uttered that I understood not; things too_ *wonderful for me, which I knew not. Hear, I beseech thee, and I will speak; I will demand of thee, and declare thou unto me. I have heard of thee by the hearing of the ear; but now mine eye seeth thee. Wherefore I abhor myself, and repent in dust and ashes.*

There it was, in black and white... *Wherefore I abhor myself, and repent in dust and ashes... Wherefore I abhor myself, and repent in dust and ashes...*

He sat back, staring off into space. Filled with the awe that comes from meeting The Holy Spirit of God face to face. *I do, Lord Jesus, I do repent in dust and ashes. I mean it. Help me undo all the awful and sinful things that have held me captive all my sorry life.* He sighed as he arose and left his room. Walking down the hall to see if Director Peter's was still awake, he knocked gently upon his door.

"Come in, Junior."

"How'd you know it was me?"

"You aren't the only one who's been on his knees. I was begging our Father God for His guidance as well as for your salvation."

Stepping into the bedroom of his counsellor, Junior reached toward his mentor, as Max reached for him. "Did you meet Jesus Christ tonight?"

"I do believe so. He led me to the section of my Bible that showed me up for what I am... or was. I actually know I've been so wrong for so long, but I now know I'm repenting for all those sins, and I really feel that he's forgiving me."

"So, you have asked Jesus to enter your heart with His Holy Spirit to provide your soul with eternal salvation?"

"Not in so many words... I just begged him to help me undo all the awful and sinful things of the past. Is that okay?"

"Sounds mighty like you truly mean business with this new life you're wanting."

"Am I supposed to feel all happy now and shout or something?"

"Why? Do you expect to feel happy? Do you feel like shouting?"

"No sir… I just thought…"

"Well, every person is different, and each individual receives God's Holy Spirit in different ways. Many do shout for joy… some cry with relief… still others simply accept the most precious gift of eternal salvation without much fanfare. But take it on blind faith, son. Continue to study your Bible every day, pray as often as you feel led to, and participate in our Sunday chapel meetings. And, will you accept the Baptism as a testament to your conversion?"

"Sure. I can remember seeing Bobby baptized back when we were kids… but I don't think he ever was converted. I know it never kept either of us from doing every dastardly deed we could get by with."

"No, I suppose not. Often times young people 'accept Jesus' on some summer night during revival just to have something exciting to do… never realizing they're living a lie to God. And, on that note… too many well-meaning preachers are quick to claim so many professions of faith, and so many baptisms during revival as a sort of rite to bragging. That in itself is sinful, and God doesn't bless such a misuse of pulpit time."

"Never thought about any of this much before. But you can bet it'll be on my mind a lot from now on. I feel as though my eyes are open and my heart too. I can barely wait to get to next Sunday's meeting. I think I'll love singing the hymns even more now." He grinned.

"Your happiness is contagious. I'm feeling pretty good about now, too. Want to see how we sound as a duet for this Sunday? I know you've got an excellent voice because I've heard you singing in the congregation. Want to surprise the men with a duet for Sunday?"

"You think we can?"

"What's to stop us. We can have something special for this Sunday as we formally welcome you into the fold of God and announce your upcoming baptism. Come on. Let's get down to the chapel without anyone else knowing… if we can." He paused, "Wait a minute. I'll put a note on my door in case."

*

The two men stepped out into the darkened hall and silently walked through the building, out the back side door and across the damp grass to the little white chapel. Entering, Max found the light switch for the choir loft and flipped it on. They strode on down to that area. "Here's the boom box. See if you can find a tape of what you'd like us to practice."

Junior went through the long, zippered case containing many of the tapes that were used for 'specials' sung by the choir. He soon found one of his favorites. "How about this one?" He handed it over to his mentor.

Max took it and slipped it into the machine… queued it up and pressed the play button. The men listened as George Beverly Shea's baritone voice rang through the little building. Both listened in rapt silence as *Just As I Am* filled the space.

As soon as it was finished, Max turned the tape over and handed one of the mikes to Junior. "Now, listen for the start of our first line."

They kept time with the introduction and right on time began singing. Oblivious to their surroundings, with eyes closed, they were vocally wide open and singing to the top of their lungs. About mid-way along in the fifth verse, Max focused his eyes downward and found the building full of men. Some in pajamas, some wrapped in bath robes, others still in full dress. The duo continued to sing until the last note faded away.

Silence…

Then resounding hooting, applause, praising, and stomping as many came rushing down front to gather around the singers. With all manner of encouragement from the listeners, the end result was that there was no way this wasn't being sung at the end of this coming Sunday's service.

Max went ahead and informed those present that Junior had indeed accepted Jesus Christ as Lord and Savior and would be formally inducted into the family of God this coming Sunday. They expected to perform his baptism soon in the small lake on the property.

After about fifteen minutes, Max was able to get everyone herded up and moved out and back toward the big building and to complete what needed to be done before lights out, since evidently the 'quiet hour' had been unsuccessful.

As he stopped at the door to his room, Max said, "Son, you're going to do just fine. God's got you now. I can relax a little bit." He smiled, "Sleep well."

"Yes'sir. Thanks. I'll probably go to sleep with that song playing in my brain for a while. I find myself almost disbelieving such a miracle has really occurred. I'll be praising God all night!" He laughed.

"We'll talk more tomorrow about your meeting with Miss Woodard."

CHAPTER 30

The Meeting

Boyd had arrived at Hope House and was ensconced in Maxwell's office. "Where are you proposing for the meeting to take place?"

"I thought the chapel might provide more security and comfort for them. There are plenty of places for the witnesses to sit as well as good acoustics for the taping. I have taken it upon myself to appoint one of our best men to record the entire thing on our video camera. I do hope Miss Woodard has been apprised that there shall be plenty of witnesses to this occasion."

"Oh, yes. I'm sure she knows everything."

"Who is accompanying her for this trip?"

"I believe Doctor Hatfield might just be with her. But, I honestly don't know for sure. They ought to be coming in any time now. When will Junior be ready?"

"Mister Raeford is already in the chapel. I believe he just might be praying for the best outcome for Miss Woodard. Let's also pray his prayers are answered."

"Indeed."

The men rose as soon as they detected foreign noises coming from the large common room. Entering the room, they found Amanda and Betty on either side of Colleen. Amanda said, "We made it at last. Sorry, it took forever to get Doctor Hatfield's permission to allow this. He was upset at first that Betty and Colleen drove down yesterday and stayed the night with me at Frank and Irene's home. I thought she'd be better there than at the hospital where everyone in town would soon find out that she's here. He soon realized I was correct in my assumption and so he prepared Betty with all the instructions to protect Colleen. For some few minutes, I actually thought he was going to come with us." She laughed.

Max stepped forward to greet Colleen, "We're so very happy to meet you, dear lady, and pray constantly for your health and safety and healing. How do you feel right now?"

Taking his hand, Colleen said, "Thank you for your prayers. I need every one of them that anyone prays for me. And I'm feeling truly fine. Not nearly as tired as I thought I might be. The trip in Amanda's car was like floating on air. I had the back seat to myself. I slept a little when I wasn't listening to the heavenly music she had for us."

"Did you rest well once you got back to Zacchary?" Boyd asked.

"Oh, yes. Mister and Mrs. Harris had every comfort imaginable. I slept like a log." She smiled, "And this morning the breakfast was wonderful. I was even allowed bacon! Haven't had bacon in ages." Looking askance at Betty, she said, "Betty tells me it isn't good for my figure."

Everyone laughed.

Director Maxwell motioned with his arms to 'gather' everyone, and said, "Does anyone have need of a restroom before we head down to the chapel for the meeting?"

"Yes. Come with me Betty. I ought to take advantage of this little respite to get my thoughts in order again… for the fiftieth time."

Max indicated the public restroom just off the hall toward the dispensary.

Boyd, Amanda, and Max stood silently waiting.

Boyd spoke, "Well, she sure looks good. Only thing to indicate she was injured is the small brace on her left hand and forearm. Other than that, she looks fine. I need to see her hair grown back out though." Then he was quick to add, "Even though she is still beautiful with her hair cut short like that."

*

The ladies soon came together with the rest of the small group, "We're ready." Said Colleen.

No other words were spoken as they walked toward the little white chapel in the near distance. Drawing closer they could hear the taped music of *"Just As I Am"* wafting from the open front door.

The group stopped short in the open foyer and held back as Colleen stepped forward into the interior of the little church building. She hesitated as she glanced down front to see three men: two strangers, and Junior. One was holding a video camera and the other was a small black man holding onto Junior's hand. She watched as Junior let go of the man's hand and took one step toward her… she watched as his face crumpled… she watched as he fell to his knees… she watched as he laid himself prone before God and her.

Suddenly, her spirit lifted itself into a realm she'd never been before. She saw a man die before her eyes. Junior was dead as sure as she was alive. He had killed himself before her. She walked down to where he lay... his body shaking, with sobs of uncontrolled sorrow... she knelt by his side and touched his back with her hand... stroked him... began to whisper, "I'm alright. Junior. I'm alright. Really. Come let me see your face again. Look at me."

Someone handed her a white handkerchief. She reached down and beneath his face to wipe his tears. "Get up, Junior. Look at me."

He reached for the handkerchief and sat up, looking into her face, "Forgive me. Oh, God, please forgive me. Colleen, forgive me."

She, still on her knees drew herself to his body and placed her arms around him and wept along with him. "You're forgiven, Junior. I know now that the person that attached me wasn't you. You could never have done it."

"But, I did. I did it!"

"No. The alcohol did it, Junior. There's a difference."

The witnesses were all weeping at the poignancy of the scene. Boyd-so grateful for this healing to begin so relatively easy... Amanda-wondering if there'd even be a prosecution in the future for Junior...Max-so thrilled to see God at work in this event... Betty-thinking that Colleen might be released from the clinic, after she talked to Doctor Bradley.

After the passage of some little time, Colleen whispered to Junior, "You've got to help me up. I'm still a little weak. Can you do it?"

He pulled back from her and stood, then literally lifted her bodily off the floor and held her in his arms for a second of so. "I promise to help you in any way you need... as often as you need. I love you."

"You can let me stand down now, Junior. They're looking at us."

He smiled and stood beside her. "She's forgiven me, Mister Peters. Just like my Heavenly Father has forgiven me."

Max stepped forward. "I have an announcement to make, friends. It's true. Junior has accepted Jesus Christ as his Lord and Savior and will be formally recognized this coming Sunday here in our chapel. I'd love to have all of you to come witness this wonderful event, and then next Wednesday, we'll have the baptism at the lake here on the property." He laughed, "Even if it's raining."

Everyone there began to shake Junior's hand, and slap him on the back, and congratulate him on his decision. "The most important decision anyone on earth can possibly make."

The men also reached to pat Colleen, hug her shoulders, and speak kind words of greeting and blessing to her. She could actually feel the love from these strangers.

Walking toward the front of the chapel, Maxwell said, "We have a very special lunch prepared for this occasion and you all are the honored guests. Come, let us not keep the men waiting any longer."

CHAPTER 31

Celebration in Zacchary

Boyd went to see Editor Willie Wilcox at the Zacchary Times to get him to write up the story for his front page. Boyd figured that the quickest way to get the word out to everyone was through the newspaper, and he wanted the town to be warned well before Colleen returned home.

Later, Amanda and Boyd found two local women- sisters, Clara and Justine Wilson who declared they were ready and able to work, and so they were taken to Colleen's little house. After the initial 'walk-through' the women soon decided where they needed to begin. The bathroom.

With all the windows and doors open to the sunshine, Boyd and Amanda, striving together, changed sheets and removed the winter drapes and hung the light spring curtains they found in the cabinet in the laundry room. Leaving the women mopping the floors, Boyd rode with Amanda in to town to pick up a few necessary items of foods for the pantry and refrigerator. While there, they dropped by the utilities office to get the electricity and gas turned on. By the time they returned to the house, LeeRoy had finished cutting the grass and was now raking the side yard.

Boyd was grateful that no neighbors stopped by to question the flurry of activity. Kids were all in school, and most everyone else was working. Only folks around were too old to care.

They locked the house, but left the yellow tape still surrounding the place to forestall any trespassers. Boyd wanted the home to be as welcoming as possible for the young woman. She'd already been through more than most people ever would and was still cresting the waves in her attempt to right her world and get back to some normalcy. He paid the two women and saw how happy they seemed to be with the amount they'd been given for the four hours of work. But they had earned every penny. Those two knew exactly what to do and how to do it and didn't waste time standing around.

Boyd figured he just might need to get them in to give the law offices a good cleaning. The jail trustees now charged with all the cleaning had become too careless and just cleaned in order to be on the legal side of the bars. The thing that bothered him most, he supposed, were the filthy windows he had to peer through each and every day. Ugh.

*

FROM DEATH TO LIFE was the headline on the front page of the Zacchary Times the next morning. Willie had written an extended account of Colleen's death and resurrection. He used every adverb available in the recounting of her death and then likewise, for her life.

By the time Colonel arrived at THE 95 late in the afternoon, the place was in a veritable uproar of celebration. "Lordy, mercy! What in th' world is a'happenin'? Has world peace been declared?"

Jolene came 'round the counter and grabbed him in a bear hug! "Colleen's comin' home! Chester! Collleen's alive and well."

He pulled away, "You outa' yore mind? Ain't no way."

"Yes! Way! Our girl was being kept safe up in some place for her to get well at." She grinned. "And, she's gonna be home in just a little while. We're planning some special celebration for when it is."

"Yeah, and I heard some truckers talkin' a little while ago about loadin' this place down with flowers for the day she's back. Everybody is tickled pink about our girl bein' alive and comin' home."

"I can't hardly believe it!" Colonel stood still as a rock. "But, somehow I just knew in my heart she was alive all the time."

"Aw, you ole' fool. You ain't thought nothin' of the sort. You was just as tore up as the rest of us when we were told she was dead and we all went to the memorial burying service. I seen you squallin' tears like rain drops... just like the rest of us."

"Well, maybe you're right, but I knowed she'd always live in our hearts anyway!" He laughed. "But, until she's here to do it herself, I need somebody to pour me a cuppacoffee! How 'bout it?"

"Sit down you crazy old man. Here, I'll pour it."

"You know I love you, don't you Jolene?"

"Yeah, yeah. We all know you love anybody what'll pour you some coffee."

The atmosphere within THE 95 was happy and every heart was filled with the joyful news. As anyone new would arrive, they were immediately given the entire story whether or not they were interested.

The restaurant was crowded... and filling up to capacity when Boyd and Amanda drove up. Cletus looked out as the car pulled into the handicapped spot. He smiled, "Looks like our Sheriff's done been arrested and handcuffed by that good lookin' Solicitor, y'all. Head's up!"

The low-pitched noise was raised by several decibels as the pair entered the area. "Welcome, Sheriff and ma'am. Looks like all our tables and booths are taken... wanna sit here at the bar?"

Boyd looked at Amanda, she grinned, "I love sitting at the bar. Have ever since I was a child and loved to go with my folks for ice cream sundaes at the drug store years ago. Yes! Let's sit at the bar."

The two friends sat as close as possible within the constraints of the stools... Heads together as they spoke in whispered words. Boyd said, "...calling Doctor Bradley first thing in the morning since you said Colleen needs to get down here as soon as she can."

"Yes. She's ready to face whatever demons lie in wait within her mind. She said Betty told her she'd stay here with her here until the appointments are established with her psychiatrist in Columbia. She's going to need company in order to feel secure... not staying in that house alone. Particularly when she learns that her son is living close by. I feel sure Betty will soothe her emotions through it all."

"We'll see." He smiled as platters were placed before them on the black marble counter, sporting big club sandwiches with all the attendant foods. "Boy, this looks so good, and I'm starving for some reason."

"I'd better not get too used to this food! I'll soon lose my girlish figure." She laughed.

Boyd looked over at her, "Ain't nothin' at all wrong with your figure, now or ever. I guess you must know you're one more beautiful lady, Amanda."

"Thank you for the kind words, Boyd." She took a large bite of the sandwich. "Let me assure you that at my age any compliment is appreciated, whether it's flattery or sincere."

"Sincerity is my middle name, didn't you know?"

They smiled into each other's eyes and busied themselves with devouring the great supper while those in attendance watched with mild wonderment as to whether their sheriff and the Solicitor were 'percolating' in the same pot.

*

Middle of the following week, Boyd got the call from Doctor Hatfield. "Yes… Wanted you to know, I have her appointments all set up… here and in Columbia. Betty's driving her down today. Guess they've been on the road a couple hours by now."

"Thanks, Doctor Hatfield. Do you know if Colleen knows yet that Bobby is living here with young Eddie?"

"From what I've been told, Nelson let her know earlier. Right after she returned to the clinic from seeing Junior. I don't know how she took that news, but you might want to let Bobby know she's on her way home. Don't know what time they'll arrive, but I'd say well before nightfall."

"Right. I'll go by there as soon as I figure they'll be home from work." As soon as he hung up the phone he thought better of the situation, so he rang Mrs. Adelaide Clark.

"Hello."

"Yes, Ma'am… Mrs. Clark. This is Sheriff Custer. Might you know about what time Mister or Mrs. Woodard get home. I need to talk with either of them, please."

Favored

"Why, yes. Yes, I do. In fact, Mister Woodard just drove up about ten minutes ago with young Eddie. They're still out in the rear yard with Jefferson. Do you want me to call him in?"

"If you don't mind, Ma'am. I need to come over there, but I want to make sure to be able to see him face to face. Can you let me speak with him just a second?"

"You just hold on, sheriff. I'll go get him right away." She laid the phone down and he could hear her shuffling away.

In just a few minutes, Boyd could hear footsteps hurrying across the room, and Eddie in the background wondering… "Is Mama alright?"

"Hold on son. I'll see… Yes'sir, Sheriff. Is something wrong?"

"Relax, son. No. Nothing is really wrong, but I need to talk with you in private for just a few minutes when you have time."

"Right now?"

"As soon as you have time."

"What's this about?"

"Well… I guess I might as well go ahead and let you know this way. I did want to see you head on, but you need to know that Colleen is headed this way… she ought to be home this evening. I don't know what you plan on doing about it, but you might want to do whatever to be prepared and to get Eddie ready too… as well as Ashe."

"Oh, my God. I'm not ready for this, even though I knew it was coming. Just pray for me and especially for Eddie. He's going to be so confused and torn up over this turn of events."

Boyd heard him as he turned away before he hung up his phone… "Come on son outside. Let's go for a ride before your mama gets home."

Bobby took his son's hand and left by the back door. Turning back, looking at his landlady, he said, "Thank you for letting me in to take the message, Ma'am."

"Is everything alright? I know it was the sheriff that called."

"Yes, Ma'am. Everything's fine."

She stood watching as Bobby spoke to Jefferson, then as he and Eddie rode off in his new-used pickup truck.

Fifteen minutes later, Ashe arrived home to find their apartment empty. She definitely remembered that Bobby had told her he was picking Eddie up early-right after school, so they could spend some time together with Jefferson down at the pond, but she's seen Jefferson out by the rose bushes raking the lawn there.

Coming down the back stairs, she ran into Adelaide. "Hello, dear. You're looking for your men, aren't you?"

"Yes, Ma'am. You wouldn't happen to know where they are, would you?"

"No, dear. I don't know that, but I do know the sheriff called to speak with your Bobby, and soon after he took Eddie with him and they rode off in the truck together."

"Sheriff?"

"Yes. Sheriff Custer."

"Thank you, Adelaide. I'll go back upstairs and give him a call to see if I can get myself satisfied about this."

*

"Oh, yes, Ma'am. I did talk with Bobby. About half an hour or so ago. I wanted to break the news to him face to face, Ma'am, but he was anxious to know, so

I just told him that Colleen is on the way back to Zacchary. She is due home this evening sometime, and I wanted him to know as much ahead of time as possible. I just found out, myself, a little while ago. I wanted him to get Eddie prepared, as well as for you two also."

"Lord! Sheriff. I knew we'd face this but something like this always comes too soon. Guess we'll just muddle through the best we can. I hope she doesn't have Bobby jailed for his kidnapping of their son. But, we'll have to take whatever is dished out to us, won't we?"

"Yes, Ma'am. We all have to live with whatever actions we make, no matter the reason. Actions have consequences."

"Yes. Well, thank you… and goodbye."

"Yes, Ma'am. Bobby asked me to pray and let me assure you that I shall. Good day to you."

*

Ashe had supper ready… holding it warm until her men arrived home again. She listened as she heard Bobby and Eddie conversing happily as they ascended the stairs. They swung open the kitchen door, and Eddie ran and threw his arms around Ashe in a tight hug. He looked up at her, and said, "I love you Mama Ashe. I'll always love you."

"So, your Daddy's told you about your mother being alive and coming home?" She looked over at Bobby, as he nodded."

"Yes'um. My Mama is coming home. Daddy told me all about how she was hurt and sent away to get better and now how she is better and ready to live here again in our little house over on Thrift Court. He said it'd be up to me as to what I want to do. That we'd all talk it out together."

He let go of Ashe, and turned, as if nothing of any importance was hanging in the air around them. "What you got that smells so good?"

Bobby and Ashe both breathed out and laughed. "Pot roast, Eddie. Been cooking low all day. Wash up and get to the table."

CHAPTER 32

The Meeting of the Year

The law complex conference room had been cleaned and prepared for the most important meeting Boyd could ever remember. The two women – Clara and Justine – had come in early Friday morning to have it done for the evening meeting. Even though it would be too dark to appreciate the fact, they washed the two windows inside and out. Boyd knew they were clean even if no one else would.

Nancy had everything ready with new tapes for the recorder. Besides which, she had two dozen fresh donuts ready and the office even sprang for a new large coffee urn from Walmart, which she'd readied with the grind she liked best. She had proudly bought a new sugar dish and had real honest-to-goodness cream in the large glass creamer. The cups were all cleaned and, even though mismatched, were of such capacity as to not need refilling but maybe once or twice during the entire meeting.

Nancy had placed all the chairs-ten of them... one extra just in case, around the polished table. She'd put a fresh tablet and government pen in front of each place along with a couple of napkins and a small paper saucer for the donuts. Thinking of Eddie, she had a Chocolate Soldier in the refrigerator.

Walking around the perimeter of the table, she envisioned Boyd at the head, with the Solicitor to his right, and Colleen on his left. Then next to her would be Betty and on to Doctor Hatfield. Bobbie would be next to the Solicitor with Eddie between himself and Ashe. Nancy herself would be down at the foot with the recorder and close to the utility table holding the refreshments.

She felt this meeting might just be the most important one she'd ever have the privilege to attend in her life. She silently prayed for an outcome to be beneficial to everyone. *Bless them all, Lord. Amen*

At seven sharp, the assorted vehicles pulled into the public lot, and Boyd, Amanda, and Nancy watched as the Ford Focus doors opened and out came Bobby, Eddie and Ashe. The doors to the other vehicle remained closed until the first trio entered the building.

Boyd stood and greeted them and had them seated on the far side of the table facing the door. He left the room and went to the outside entrance to meet the next trio of folks. "Good evening. The others are already seated and are waiting. Y'all ready?" And he looked directly at Colleen.

She smiled brightly, "Yes, indeed, Sheriff. I am more than ready to get this over and done with so we can all get on with our lives."

"Come on in. First door here on your right."

Colleen was first to enter the room and Bobby stood immediately, but he restrained his son with a hand upon his upper arm. The boy sat silent... wide eyed... tears flooding down his cheeks.

Colleen could hear his silent pleas... *Mama. Mama.* She smiled and winked at him and nodded. "It's alright, son." She said.

Soon, the entire group was seated. Everyone looked to Boyd, who looked first to everyone around the table and motioned for Nancy to activate the recorder. He began, "Friends, we know why we're here this evening. For the record, it's April 16th, 1999. Those present are..." and he proceeded to name each person at the table. Turning to Amanda, he said, "Now, I'd like to turn this meeting over to our Solicitor, Amanda Harris. She has a prepared statement for all to know and understand before we get any further along with this."

Amanda nodded, and said, "First thing... I want to know if Colleen needs to say something before the proceedings begin."

Colleen stood from her seat and walked around to the other side of the table and reached out for Bobbie to release Eddie. The child then stood and swept himself into her arms as she knelt before him. They held each other as Colleen kept shushing her son from wanting to cry out. After a few seconds, she reached and wiped his face with a handkerchief from her pocket, then finally, she pulled him from her close grasp and looked him in the eyes... "Darling Eddie. Soon we grown-ups will work everything out for good. Until then you must sit here by your father and just try to understand everything that's going to be going on around you for a little while. You're going to need to trust us all. Do you understand?"

"I guess so, Mama. I'll try." Then as she rose from kneeling, Eddie grabbed her neck again and said, "I love you, Mama. I love you."

As soon as Colleen and Eddie were seated once again, Amanda spoke, "From everything I can gather concerning you, Colleen, I want to simply place it all before this group today for benefit of edification. Number one. Your son was kidnapped by his father around three years ago, is that correct?"

"Yes." Replied Colleen.

"Alright. Number two. You filed for and were granted a divorce about a year after your husband left, is that correct?"

"Yes."

"Good. Then I must inform you that you hold within your power the ability to charge him with kidnapping. Think about this for a few minutes while I lay the rest of this out." She went on, "Number three. You, Colleen, were kidnapped, raped, and attacked on January 8th of this year. Is this correct?"

"Yes."

Bobby stood, but Boyd looked at him and motioned him to sit.

Amanda cleared her throat and said, "You now have the power, Colleen, to press charges to the fullest extent of the law against your husband for the kidnapping of your son, but also against your attacker." She looked around at everyone and continued, "Not only did you survive the assault, you are pregnant from the rape."

Bobby, nearly knocked over his chair when he stood again. "Boyd then jumped up... "Sit down Mister Woodard. Don't make me throw you into a cell for safekeeping! You'd better not interrupt this hearing again. Do I make myself clear?"

Bobby slammed himself back down into his chair and threw his head down upon his crossed arms on the conference table. Ashe reached over to stroke his back, and he shrugged her hand away.

"Continue, Amanda."

"I've said all of the fore-going, so everyone can realize what this victim has faced and is in the process of overcoming and trying to work through. Please, allow her to take whatever time is necessary to address her concerns without interruption."

The table was silent as Betty and Doctor Hatfield watched Colleen's countenance race through the gamut of emotions. Finally, they all heard her audible inhalation of a deep breath. Still they held.

"Friends. Thank you all for coming here to meet with me for these very important, life-changing decisions." She hesitated, then went on. She looked directly at Bobby as he raised up to watch her. "I know you've been caught between a rock and a hard place Bobby, but this is exactly where you've placed yourself by stealing my son."

Eddie had begun to weep gently when the lady was numbering off the things that had befallen his mother. He never knew she'd been through so much. *I'll make it right, Mama.* He thought.

Then Colleen, looked directly at her boy, "Eddie, from everything I can see, I do believe your father loves you and has taken very good care of you. From my perspective, I now believe it may have been best for you that you weren't with me when I was attacked. I don't know what might have become of you if you'd been home with Carrie, waiting for me." She looked at Ashe. "For that I'm grateful." She then continued, "But, I'd like my son to be reinstated into my care, full time. How soon can this be arranged?"

"Since young Eddie was forcefully taken by the illegal act of kidnapping, you have the power to take him home with you tonight. It's totally up to you."

"Well, I won't do that. I know his father and step-mother will want to get sorted out and everything. They'll need to prepare him for the change in his life. And, besides, I'll need to get a job to be able to take care of him." She paused. "There's a lot more involved in bringing my son back home than I considered. He mustn't be removed from school for even a day. I don't want his life too interrupted for my benefit. His needs must be first and foremost."

Ashe spoke up for the first time. "Mrs. Woodard, might I suggest that until you're ready for your son to live with you full time that we leave everything as is. We have him in private school up in Summerton because we thought it best for him to have the finest education we could possibly provide. He could simply visit you each weekend until time for the full move. That way he could get used to the idea and so could we. What do you think?"

Before she could answer, Bobby spoke up, "I'd continue to pay for his schooling and give you whatever you need to live on until such time as you get ready to take on a full-time job."

"You're making it mighty difficult for me to press charges aren't you, Bobby?" She looked dead serious.

"Do what you want to as far as I'm concerned, but I'll support you as long as I'm allowed to work. I cannot do that behind bars."

"I'm no fool, Bobby. I realize I'm in somewhat of a quandary with my situation as well as being pregnant. I don't know whether or not I'll be able to hold down a full-time job anyway. I don't even know where to begin looking for something where I can make what I was pulling in out at THE 95."

"I might be speaking out of turn, but I know the crew out there are chomping at the bit for your return. It'd be up to you as to whether or not you could stay on your feet and work the hours you did in the past… but I'd be willing to bet my new car that you'd be able to work any way you'd need to; any time you'd need to." Said Amanda.

"Then, I guess it's settled. I'll leave things like they are for the present. But…" She looked at Eddie, "I need to be with him as much as I can."

"How about we let him go with you and your nurse now. Bobby and I can run home and get clothes for the weekend, and you can have him ready for Bobby to come by and pick him up on Monday for school on his way to work. How does that sound?"

Colleen fought the tears back and replied, "Sounds wonderful." Looking at her son, she asked, "Would you like to come with me to spend the weekend?"

He looked to his father and Ashe questioningly, and finally back to his mother, and nodded, "Yes ma'am, I would, if it's alright."

The meeting began to wind down with everyone getting up for coffee and Nancy laid out the big plate of donuts for everyone. She retrieved the Chocolate Soldier for Eddie, and he was thrilled. "I was afraid I wasn't going to get anything but water to drink." Everyone laughed as the tension was relieved.

Privately Amanda told Boyd she suspected that ultimately Colleen wouldn't charge Bobby at all, and she then said, "And you know, I seriously doubt if she'll even charge Junior for his role in her life. She's connected to him by that baby."

"Yeah. It's something to wonder about… how it's all going to pan out."

*

Within a week Colleen had been out to visit THE 95 half a dozen times. Each time Milford asked her when she would be able to come back to work. She never gave him a definite answer but kept promising that it'd be sooner than later. Then on the Friday that Bobby brought Eddie out there where they were to meet Colleen, she told him that she had been working nearly all day and was ready to get home.

"Wow! You're already strong enough to make the all-day hours?"

"So far, but, I'm really worn out. At least I didn't get sick like I feared I would. Remember when I was so sick with Eddie? Ugh! It's the worst part of pregnancy."

As they walked out toward the vehicles, Bobby asked, "What're you planning to do about Junior?"

"That's the question of the century, isn't it? I find myself vacillating between several different scenarios." She laughed. "Everything from hanging him by the neck in the town square to picturing him blindfolded before a firing squad with my rifle being the one holding the bullet, to seeing him driving mules through old man Spearman's pasture. You remember how he used to hate his summers there working the fields. I've got to admit that having the power of life and death over someone is heady, indeed. But, I spend most of my time seeking what God would have me do… particularly since I'm carrying his child."

"All I can tell you, Colleen, is that I do sincerely say the words… 'I am so sorry'… but I know words are cheap. I'll gladly take whatever you decide without any backtalk at all. I was thinking only of myself when I took Eddie. I wasn't even considering the damage I was doing to you, let alone to him."

"No, I don't think you were using your head at all, but I'm grateful to Ashe for being the mother to my son that she has been. I do think Eddie loves her as his mother. That says a lot about his contentment now. I believe children are resilient in most every way and will come through most traumas without the heavy baggage that grownups tend to grab hold of. I admire how you've taken to doing what you believe is best for him and his future. Like the Academy. Just wish I could have afforded to install him there from the beginning of his schooling. But, at least he's there now. And getting a good education, from everything I could find out about the school. For that I thank you, Bobby."

"Here… I'll get his bag."

"See you bright and early on Monday, Bobby."

He waved to his son, patiently waiting in Colleen's little car. Eddie smiled and waved back. "Bye, daddy."

CHAPTER 34

Opening the Sealed Box

Monday morning, Boyd was halfway with his rump to meeting the black leather of his desk chair when Nancy rushed in. "Take this call now, Boss... Sheriff... It's Junior's psychiatrist. I forget his name."

Boyd sat and reached for the phone, punched the lit button and spoke, "Sheriff Custer here. What can I do for you?"

"Good morning, Sheriff. This is Christian Taylor. I am the Doctor in charge of the young man you have incarcerated out at Hope House... A William Travis Raeford, Jr."

"Yes. What can I do for you, sir?"

"I'd like to meet with you and your Solicitor as soon as you can find time to get here. It appears to me, at least, that the prisoner has begun recovering much of the lost memory of the events surrounding the attack. I'd like to get everything as soon as possible in case he begins to regress and lose what seems to be surfacing. I don't want him traumatized, but neither do I want to lose this opportunity to expose these memories so we can help him understand and overcome them."

"Yes! Yes. I'll contact the Solicitor and will call to let you know as soon as I know we're on the way. This is the best I can do. I want to get this case wound up and maybe this'll do it for us."

"I'll be waiting for your call… at least, call Maxwell."

"Will do. And, thank you."

*

Amanda swung the car into the lot and slammed out of it and ran toward the building… she met Boyd headed out. Without thinking, she opened her arms and drew him into a tight hug! "Oh, Boyd… maybe this'll be what we need to close this case out."

He laughed. "Now, let's not get carried away yet! Removing himself from her embrace, he took her arm and headed to the cruiser."

Once they were well on the way, Amanda spoke up. "Wonder how this Doctor was able to pull this information from his brain? I've heard of a number of cases where such information is lost forever… the person dies without ever having recovered the memories."

"I don't know anything about this sort of thing. In fact, I never knew anything could be so lost into the mind so as not to be retrievable, but maybe it's all our prayers. Who knows. I just hope we can close all the gaps of the events and get some valid picture of exactly what did transpire that night."

"Me too."

By four that afternoon, the cruiser pulled up to the front of the building. Several men were busy in the front yard, sprucing it up. They all nodded to the couple and spoke gentle greetings as the pair walked up the steps, across the wide porch, and entered the cool interior. They headed directly toward Maxwell's office and knocked on the door.

A voice inside bade them come on in. Max stood and said, "Well. You made good time. Surely you didn't break any speed laws, now did you Boyd?"

Another man arose from his chair. Both Amanda and Boyd knew Max, but the other was a stranger. He stepped forward with hand outstretched. "I'm Doctor Christian Taylor. I believe it was you, Sheriff, that I spoke with early this morning?"

"Yes sir, very pleased to meet you," and stepping aside he reached for Amanda, "This is our Solicitor, Amanda Harris."

Amanda shook hands with the Doctor and asked, "How is your patient doing today?"

"He's reclaimed a great deal of the lost memories. At least, from everything I've been able to ascertain. Thus far, I do have all of our sessions on record, so as he's speaking we'll know if it's old or new recollections."

"Where is he now?"

"In my office with my assistant. Max provides a room for all the Doctors who donate their time to this work. I just happen to be proficient in this particular field of the mind. Maxwell brought me in a couple of weeks ago in the hopes I'd be able to access this patient's past. I'm happy to report that so far, so good. Would you like us to visit with him now?"

The foursome walked down the hall, past the dispensary toward a door with a small window containing a sliding door behind white-painted bars. Amanda noted the heavy locking system… however it was easily swung open and they entered.

Junior swept off the cot and grabbed Boyd in a bear hug. "I'm remembering everything, Boss… I mean Sheriff. Everything!" he stepped back and toward Amanda, "Pleased to see you again, Ma'am. Tell me how Colleen's doin'?"

"She's fine, Junior. I'll give her your regards."

Doctor Taylor placed his hand upon Junior's shoulder and bade him seat himself upon the cot once more. The other's found seats toward the perimeter of the small room.

Boyd nodded in acknowledgement to the Doctor's assistant- a muscular young man in white with a crew cut. Boyd noted how kind the expression upon his face appeared. He was big, but he was benevolent… the two words: *gentle giant*, came into his mind. *I suppose he might come in handy in cases when a patient wants to get out of hand.* He thought.

Taylor seated himself in a straight chair next to the head of the cot. He then reached forward to indicate the assistant. "This is my assistant, Michael Angelo… and don't laugh, folks. His parents had a great sense of humor and they passed it on to my right-hand man." He smiled.

"Yes, sir. He's correct. I've grown skin as thick as alligator hide ever since I was a kid. Kinda become used to my moniker now, though. Y'all can call me Mike."

The room laughed gently, and Boyd watched as Junior grinned from ear to ear. "Mike is my kinda man, ya'll. He's been through a lot too, and's doing fine. I think I'll probably make it outa these dark woods too."

"Well, William… You know you're in the company of people who love you. No one will think anything harshly of whatever you expose to us this day. How is the comfort level with where you find yourself this moment?"

"Just thinking about what all I'm remembering scares the tar out'a me, but I've enough sense left to know too that it all needs to be exposed to the light of day, so I can face everything and get better. I already know I more or less killed the woman I love with all my heart, along with raping her. Just the recalling of the events during those hours cannot hurt more than I'm already facing so if it'll help to tie up this bag of mess, then so be it. I'm ready to tell everything I can."

"Now, William, we're going to darken the room somewhat to help in your concentration. Get comfortable on the cot." Looking around he said, start the tape now… it's already been queued up with the date and the occasion. Please, no speaking or interruptions, unless an emergency arises. The phone has been disconnected also. Woolsey is standing guard down the hall to maintain quiet for us." He stood by Junior, leaned over and spoke quietly… take us back to the first thing you can recall about what happened."

"Yes, sir. I'm just going to say stuff as it comes into my head. I think the beginning was when I happened to look out and see Colleen stop by the dumpster out behind the complex in that wide alleyway. You know which one I'm talking about, Sheriff. Anyway, I saw her get out of her little car and carry a large black plastic bag over and throw it into the dumpster. After she drove off I was curious, so I went and pulled the bag out. Being as how it's near the impound, I quickly took it over and threw it into the back of the impounded pickup that's been there forever. Anyway, at lunch time I went out and opened the bag and saw it full of old stuff that I figured had belonged to Bobby… even some boots that still looked plenty good… enough for hunting and fishing anyway. So, I had the bright idea to take some of the things to use for that… hunting and fishing, you know, specially since we're the same size. I took the clothes I chose and stuck them in the cab of the truck and threw the rest of them that were still in the bag back into the dumpster.

As you know, Sheriff, that old pickup ought to've been auctioned off, but that's beside the point. I took to keeping extra bottles of liquor beneath the front seat, and when I felt like it, I'd sneak out and have a swig as often as I could get by with it. I don't rightly know if anyone knew I had begun drinking heavily again. I think I must have been covering my butt pretty good because nobody ever said anything.

But I think seeing Colleen that morning at the dumpster set my heart on fire. I was madder'n hell about her picking Bobby over me. Guess I've never gotten over it. The more I thought about how she'd spurned me for Bobby, the madder I got and the more I drank. I stayed away from the office on one excuse or another until Sheriff Boyd left. By late that evening I hardly recall what I was thinking. I just know I took the truck out of impound and drove out to THE 95 to watch for Colleen to get off work. I can now remember that I figured if I dressed in Bobby's clothes, she'd be happy to see me. So, I changed there in the truck and put on his dungarees and shirt. There was even one of his belts on the pants. I put on his boots too, even though they were a size or two too large, I didn't care.

I stood in the shadows near her car and waited. By the time she came out I was positive she'd be happy to see me thinking I was Bobby that'd been gone all that time. But as I reached for her she knew I wasn't Bobby right off... pulling away and I could see she was getting ready to scream. I grabbed her throat to shut off the scream and when she fainted I dragged her over to the truck and shoved her inside. She came to as I climbed into the driver's side, so I slammed her head against the dashboard so hard she fainted again. I guess. Anyway, she shut up. As I drove away she slid down into the floorboard and lay there without making a sound. I drove, and I don't know how I chose where I ended up. I think I was driving blind. I finished another bottle and as soon as she'd whimper I hit her with the full one that was laying on the seat next to me.

Finally, I decided to stop the truck and I came around to get her out from the floorboard. I think I just grabbed her arm and pulled her out. I know she did not resist me, so I halfway thought she might be dead. I dragged her for however long it was and started to dig a hole to bury her when she came to again. I wanted to see her body so bad. I tried to get her clothes off, but she kept crying and fighting, so I hit her with a limb that found its' way into my hand. She shut up then. I decided to cut her jeans off. I remember seeing the blood seeping out from where the knife cut her legs. I became so enraged until I literally tore the blouse off and I cut the front of her brassiere in two. By then I had torn my – or Bobby's clothes off and then I remember reaching to tear the crotch of her panties and I raped her.

After I finished, I grabbed all the clothes and put them aside. I dug a hole as big as I thought I needed to hide her body and then I covered her with leaves. I picked up the boots and found all the clothes I could find and began running through the woods. I have no idea of where I went or anything, but I stumbled somewhere so I started digging and tried to get everything covered up. I was still in my shorts, so I took them off and flung them into the trees. I guess maybe all that stuff is still out there somewhere. Then I saw the boots I forgot to bury, so I put them back on. Other than the boots, I was naked and freezing. I just began running back toward the lights of town not even thinking of where I was, but I guess I'd come out onto the hunter's road and happened to come upon the pickup where I'd left it. I put my uniform back on and drove back to the impound, left the truck, and walked home carrying my own shoes and socks in my hand.

Next morning, I still had my uniform on and the strange boots. I wondered where my shorts were. I had to strip the bed because there was dirt everywhere. I hardly thought about it. It seems that since I've been on the bottle so much that I lose memory, but every day I tell myself that it's the last drink I'll ever take. Anyway, after I showered and shaved, I took the boots and threw them into the dumpster at work. Never knowing what I had done, so help me God. To the best of my ability, I do believe this is what happened that night."

Silence.

Doctor Taylor reached and laid his hand upon Junior's shoulder and nodded. "Thank you, William. Thank you."

Max asked, "Might we turn up the lights now?"

"Yes. Go ahead." Looking to Junior, he said, "Sit up now and keep your eyes closed until you feel you can face the brightness. It won't make any difference in how rested you now feel. Help him Mike."

Mike lifted Junior to a sitting position and kept himself next to the patient on the narrow cot. He placed a large arm around the shoulders of Junior and said, "You can open your eyes now, friend."

Junior smiled, "Did you get it all, Doctor?"

"Yes, William, I do believe you've unwound the tangled knot-as you so aptly say. There were even additions that you'd not spoken before."

"Lordy, Junior. You've been carrying around a bundle of burdens for too long, son. I'm glad you've finally gotten this out, so you and the good Doctor can deal with everything and get you totally healed." Said Boyd.

"What will you do now that you know everything?" Asked Junior.

Amanda spoke up and said, "As before, everything is in the hands of Colleen. She is the only one who can and must make such decisions. You will be apprised as soon as it's all settled to her satisfaction. None of us have any suspicion as to how she ultimately will conclude her desires. Just know, we shall abide by her wishes in this case."

"She ought to have me hung!"

"No, Mister Raeford. You forget that you are the father of her child. Colleen must do what she deems best for herself and her baby. Don't forget that."

"No Ma'am. I had though, for a moment. I just hope she won't hold it against the baby because of what I did."

"Surely you can't believe she would. If you think that, then you certainly do not know the woman you accosted. She has proven to be one of the strongest, most understanding, insightful persons I've ever come across. Rest assured… Colleen will weigh all her options and certainly will know she must live her future and that of her child with the decisions she makes about this."

"She's correct, William. Your future too, rests upon those decisions. However, we at Hope House will do everything in our power to see that you can access some semblance of normalcy no matter what her ultimate terms are. If prison-then you shall accept it with the assurance that it won't last forever. You find yourself presently at the best of crossroads to step into your future."

"How's that?"

"First and foremost, you are a child of God-saved by His grace. Then you are clean of your need of alcohol… forever. And certainly not last, but once you serve whatever sentence might be imposed, you shall be free to enjoy life wherever that might be."

"… And still will be a young man with many years ahead of you." Said Mike.

Junior smiled. "Well, I am anxious to complete my time here, serve my time in prison, and try to figure out what I will do for a living for the remainder of my time here on earth."

"Good plan, Son." Said Boyd, standing. "It's time we headed back to Zacchary. Is there anything else you need from us?"

"Just wait until I get the copy of the tape ready. You'll want that."

"Oh, yes. Thanks."

"Please excuse me, gentlemen." Looking at Boyd, she said, "I'll meet you in the great room."

Boyd reached to hug Junior and whispered, "Son, do everything you can to stay on the right track and leave everything to Colleen. She's not dumb nor is she vindictive. Rest in whatever she decides, as it'll be best for everyone concerned. I have a feeling. Okay?"

"Yes'sir, I will. I promise by God's grace that I'll ever be the man you'd want as you would for your own son."

Boyd smiled, knowingly.

Everyone vacated the room and were standing in the large room at the center of the facility when Amanda came toward them. All eyes were upon her svelte figure as she walked… each with his own thoughts about the beautiful woman.

Boyd reached and took her arm in a small show of possession… "This way, Madam. We've a long way to go."

They waved slightly as they left the building… being observed until they drove off.

*

"I intend to stay here in Zacchary until Colleen makes up her mind. I promise I won't push her toward any conclusion. It must not be forced, and I want you to promise me you won't hint at anything either."

"No, I won't. Besides, I won't be with her without you being there anyway." He indicated the little box of recorded tapes on the seat between them. "You lettin' Colleen hear what happened to her?"

"Not on your life. There's no need for her to ever be tainted by knowing this. Now, if she ever remembers anything it'll be her problem, but I don't think she ever will. She was unconscious most of the attack anyway. So, I think she'll be safer without this… just be sure to lock it in with the evidence downstairs."

*

That evening Boyd drove out to THE 95 and was greeted heartily by the crew. Colleen stepped around the counter and reached to hug him. "Where's your girlfriend?"

Boyd smiled, "Would you believe she preferred to take supper with her in-laws tonight? Of course, they told her they'd invited a dozen or so intimate friends to dinner. She told me she couldn't refuse them. She did say, though, that she'd rather have the grub here anytime… if that makes y'all feel better!"

Colleen walked him over to a booth, but he shook his head. "Naw, let me sit at the bar… closer to my friends that way."

"Sure, Sheriff. Come on. Sit right here by the register. What'll you be havin' this evening?"

"Bein' as how it's Monday, I know Cletus has something extra special ready. I'll just have whatever that is, along with a big glass of iced tea."

Colleen scurried around and quickly placed the large glass of sweet tea in front of him, then Jolene laid down a big, flat saucer filled with salad greens, topped with boiled egg slices and spring onion pieces, topped with a dollop of Ranch. As Boyd dug into the salad, Colleen placed a napkin-wrapped chunk of toasted, Italian garlic bread nearby. Lastly, Cletus brought out the deep platter of spaghetti with hearty meat sauce piled over the top. "Eat up, Sheriff.

I know it's mighty warm tonight for such fare as this, but our Truckers look for this every Monday… and besides it's cool in here. Enjoy!"

Nodding, with his mouth full, he waved his fork into the air and kept on eating.

A few other patrons were quietly talking throughout the rest of the restaurant, but 'the crew' were all looking directly at Boyd. He soon became aware that he was being scrutinized. "What?"

"Oh, you know. We got wind that you and that Amanda lady were up to Hope House today to see Junior."

"My God! How in the Sam Hill did y'all find out about that? This place is worse than some girls dormitory! News in Zacchary travels faster than lightnin' across the sky! Good grief." And he took another mouthful.

"Well?"

"Well, nothing! None of y'all need to know anything about police business, but just to allay your fears… Junior is fine. He's coming along good in his treatment." Looking at Colleen… "We're all holding our breaths on everything until our girl here comes to the decision of what she wants to do about him. That's all."

"I'm sorry, Sheriff. I know I'm dragging my feet, but I've got so much to consider first. The lives of four people are in this mess and I'm the only one holding the ultimate outcome of us all."

"I know, Honey. You just take your time. Nobody's rushing you… not even Junior. And by the way, he sends you his regards, for what that's worth."

"It means a lot to me, Sheriff. It means a lot. Thanks."

*

Time inexorably marched on with very few changes, except in the case of Colleen's pregnancy. Doctor Hatfield had set her up with a regimen of appointments and a plethora of vitamins and stringent instructions to follow.

In spite of those restrictions she became somewhat content with her lot in life. Having her son with her every Friday after school, until she had him dressed and ready for his father to pick him up on Monday was as fulfilling as it was harrying. She'd rearranged her little house to accommodate a private little room for him next to the only bathroom in the house. He did his homework each Friday at the little kitchen table-where Colleen learned more about his school subjects than she thought possible. Reading geography books and delving into American History tomes, and calling his spelling words out several times improved her own knowledge. Grateful for small favors, she reveled in every moment of his presence.

Milford was bending over backward to see that Colleen worked as much as she was able to during the week, so she could be at home every weekend. No one out at THE 95 complained about the cushy hours of their compatriot.

Several times during those weeks, Ashe would send Bobby to pick up Colleen from work to bring her out to their apartment for a dinner meal. Being in such surroundings, Colleen was able to see Eddie's comfort with his father and step-mother. Grateful beyond words, she slowly made up her mind to continue the visitation as it presently was… even after-particularly after the baby came. But, she never capitulated so far as to let the Judge make it permanent. They'd just rock on as it was. Colleen never was bothered by the unsettled nature of the 'visitation' being unfair to Bobby. After all, he had his son more than most men would in his situation. He could be in prison for kidnapping if Colleen chose.

*

Junior made such strides in his treatment until Max called Boyd to see if he wouldn't allow Junior to be released from his restrictions. This request prompted Boyd to contact Colleen.

"Afternoon Colleen. I'm headed out your way for lunch. You free to talk a little while I'm there?"

"Sure. I'll be here until around quarter to three. Bobby will come by the house about then to bring Eddie. You come on. I'll have your tea ready."

*

Removing his broad-brimmed hat, Boyd said, "Afternoon, folks. How is everybody this hot May afternoon?"

Selma spoke up… "Git on in here where it's cool and take a seat. You want the counter?"

Boyd nodded. Colleen set the big sparkling glass of sweet iced tea in front of him. "You want the barbeque today?"

Grinning, "You know I do."

While absentmindedly wiping the counter in front of the Sheriff, Colleen finally asked, what do you need to talk with me about today?"

"Wait 'til the 'cue gets here. Gimme time for a taste or two… then, I'll be up to askin' you a couple of questions. No big deal… just tryin' to keep myself up on everything. Need a minute to think."

While Boyd dug into the plateful of food, Colleen busied herself with serving other diners. After a few minutes she found herself back in front of the

Sheriff. "You need to ask me whatever it is. I need to take a break in about ten minutes. Milford makes me take breaks every so often."

"Sure." He leaned back a tad, and spoke, "How'd you feel about seeing Junior again? He has been under heavy surveillance and locked up every night since we knew he attacked you. He needs to stay up in Hope House until Mister Peters deems he's ready to be let out on his own. We cannot do that. He must be incarcerated until such time as you determine we can prosecute him for the crimes he's committed. I figure you might want to let us and him know what you want to do."

Tears began to form in her eyes. "I know, Sheriff. I've been praying for God to tell me what He wants me to do, but so far nothing definite has come to me."

"In that case, it would appear to me that God is leaving it totally up to you. He must know you already have enough knowledge of your condition, the condition of Junior, as well as Eddie and the baby. It's time for you to step up and make the move you know in your heart is the right one. It's already there, Colleen. You and I both know it. Isn't that right?"

Large tears slipped across her lower eyelids and dropped down her cheeks as she nodded. "You're right, Sheriff. I've been knowing what I need to do, but I realize too, that I've been arguing with God about it for quite a while." She wiped her face with her ever-present handkerchief. "Just let me know when you want to take me up to see Junior. I'll get Milford to let me off."

Laying a twenty on the counter, Boyd rose, "I'll call you soon." He walked to the end of the counter and reached for Colleen. She went into his arms. "I hate I pushed you, but I know you're ready to close this out and get on without this cloud hanging over your head. You'll be able to breathe better now. Call me."

*

Amanda insisted on driving the three of them that Thursday morning. The week before, Betty had reluctantly returned to the mountain clinic and for the initial hours after she left, Colleen wept… wept until Friday when Bobby dropped by with her son. Since with his presence each weekend, his mother had improved both mentally as well as physically. Today she was feeling better than she had since before the attack. She'd spent her waking hours in prayer for this meeting. She was ready. Mind made up as to what she intended to do. She was sure. She'd mentally set the matter in concrete and greeted the day with a light heart.

"Shall I sit in the back?"

"Only if you desire. You might be more comfortable back there." Said Amanda. "Especially since Boyd is driving!"

"What? Me drive this thing?" He grinned. "No way." He shook his head. "No, Amanda, you drive. You can let me drive later when we've more time and not on official business."

She laughed. "Oh. You mean on some back, out of the way roads?"

"Now, that'd be right up my alley." He grinned.

Amanda open the passenger door for Colleen. "If you insist, then… Boyd you sit in back, so Colleen can sit up here with me."

"Fine by me. That way I can keep my eye on you two girls."

"Yeah… and you cannot see the speedometer!"

They laughed as they settled themselves and drove away from Colleen's little house. Everyone in a very happy and festive mood.

*

Several men were sitting on the wide front porch when the sporty black car pulled to the front and stopped. Colleen looked out as she opened the door and stepped into the arms of Junior. "Boy! Am I happy to see you. I know I'm not supposed to react to your presence like this, but I can't help myself. You look so beautiful. You feelin' alright?"

Stepping back from the embrace, Colleen smiled, "Yes. I'm doing much better. How about you?"

The group walked to the house and were greeted by Maxwell. "Glad you got here so quickly. Lunch is ready to be served and we don't want to hold the servers back from their jobs. Anyone need the restroom before we head in?"

They went in different directions for the restrooms and within minutes were back in the great room and headed into the huge dining hall. As they entered, every eye was trained upon the group and they were greeted profusely as honored guests. Shown to the head of the line. It was common knowledge that an important meeting was about to transpire… that held the future of one of their own.

Six seated themselves at a table near the section farthest away from the serving line and the apart from the heart of noise. Boyd, Colleen, Amanda, Junior, Woolsley, (who'd been assigned as the monitor of Junior since he'd been under house arrest) and the Director. Max bade God's blessing upon their meal and then spoke, "Sheriff, we're so very happy to have you here today. I think it's particularly appropriate to announce that we're having a graduation ceremony this upcoming Sunday evening. Junior will graduate from Hope House with my blessing. He has more than fulfilled all the requirements and is, without doubt, ready to reenter society."

"What time of evening?" Asked Colleen.

"The ceremony will take place in the chapel at seven." He looked around the table, "I do hope you all will be able to celebrate this occasion with us." And as if it were the abiding reason, he added… "Of course, we'll have dinner before meeting in the chapel."

Boyd nodded. "I'll sure be here for this. How long's it been Junior?"

"Right at four months. And they've flown by." Looking at his mentor, "Director keeps us busy and the time flies." He laughed, "And I've even learned how to milk a cow!"

They all laughed.

Boyd squelched an unholy desire to tell Junior that he hoped he enjoyed it as he'd never get the chance to fondle tit's that big again!

Colleen spoke… shattering the picture in Boyd's head. "I'd like to come if I can bring Eddie with me. Would it be alright to bring him? He's nine. I think he'd like to witness something like this graduation."

"Absolutely. I'm sure young Eddie will enjoy meeting these men and seeing the formality and seriousness of the graduation ceremony."

"Think he'll remember me?" Asked Junior.

"Of course, he will. After all you and his daddy were together nearly all the time before he was taken away."

"Oh, Colleen. If I could only take back all those terrible days from my past, I would. The only thing I can say is I promise to God and this company and mostly to myself, that such behavior is past and shall never surface again. God has truly given me a new lease on my life. I have been provided with new eyes and a new heart that sees through His Spirit Veil to view my world in a totally different way from what I've ever experienced before, or ever knew was possible. As my Bible tells me… my old man is dead, and my new man belongs to my Father God."

The group sat in silence… with reverent awe as they witnessed first-hand the sincerity espoused by this once-broken man.

"Junior will give his testimony on Sunday night. It's something you don't want to miss, if you can find the time to make the trip. I know it's quite a drive but might just be worth the effort."

"Would you like me to try to get word to your mother?"

"If you think she might want to make the trip. I haven't heard from her in nearly a year, as best as I can recall. She might not even be where she was then."

"I'll see if I can find out where she is for you. I know she'd want to be here."

"Thanks, Sheriff. It'd sure make my turn in life complete if mother could be with us. But, I won't be disappointed too much if she can't. Somehow, I believe she sorta felt she could get on with her life once she saw I was so close to you. Almost as if you took over for my father in her eyes. Know what I mean?"

A chill ran through Boyd, as he contemplated the words of this young man. He was as sure as his name was Boyd Custer that Junior was his biological son, and that Mazie knew it too.

After lunch they left the dining hall and entered Maxwell's office. He closed the door, but not before the 'do not disturb' sign was hung on the handle.

Finding seats for everyone-including Woolsley, Maxwell didn't sit behind the desk but pulled his chair, so they were seated in a loose circle. He reached over and held Junior's hand. "Son, this is one of the most important days to ever occur in your life. No matter what is forthcoming in the next few minutes you have total control over how you respond. I don't need to warn you of anything. You've brains enough to understand certain obligations must be met. Meet whatever comes like the man God made you to be."

Junior smiled, nodded, and looked directly at Colleen… waiting.

She glanced at Amanda…

"It's your time, Colleen. Use it wisely."

She silently asked God for His blessing on her decision. "Thank you all for being here with me as I take this time to speak about the power I alone have over the life of another. Just as Junior spoke earlier about how God infiltrated his life to bring him to where he finds himself now, God certainly held on to me during the difficult times I've come though… no, the difficult times that God has brought me through. The final outcome of today is truly led by the Spirit of God. He is the one at play in this hour."

She then reached over and took Junior's hand. "Look at me, Junior. These words now shall affect our lives, and those around us from now on, so don't think for a moment that I haven't given them some serious consideration. It boils down to the fact, that the other night down in the Chapel when we held each other, and you begged for forgiveness… I recall my words in reply. I told you then that I forgave you. I have not, nor ever will change my mind. Just as you know you aren't the man you once were before God forgave you… neither am I the woman I once was… capable of vindictiveness against my tormentors. Not just you, Junior, but Bobby too. I firmly believe God chose for us to live through these horrific times in order that we may be brought through the fire to emerge far beyond what we could ever have imagined ourselves capable of becoming. I believe He is at the core of our existence now and shall remain so."

Junior dropped his head and wept heavy tears of relief. Colleen stuffed her handkerchief into his hand. She then looked to Sheriff Boyd… Amanda,

"I now formally refuse to prosecute this man and I do hold him blameless for any previous action he committed against me."

There was heavy silence as the pronouncement hung in the still air.

Amanda spoke, "I'm not even going to question your decision. I shall dispose of this case as though it never occurred."

Breaking the tension, Boyd stood and reached for the hand of Junior. "God has blessed you son, don't forget it."

He raised up… "You don't worry, sir."

Max said, as the rest stood from their chairs. "Would you care for some cold drinks before you head back to Zacchary? There's plenty of iced tea and water out front in the great room."

Walking into the front area, Junior reached for Colleen and strode closely beside her. With head bent down near to her, he said, "You know I've always loved you, don't you?"

"I do know that, Junior. There's just no understanding why our lives took the turns they did… but I refuse to try to second guess that era. My life is different now… my attitude, my hopes are all seen in the light of what's best for all of us instead of just for myself. I've changed, too."

"Are you going to be here for my graduation?"

"Sure going to try. I'll bring Eddie too… and thinking about it-would you like me to invite Bobby and Ashe?"

"Wow! Never thought about that. If you think they'd come, I'd be tickled to see them here too."

"I'll get Sheriff to call Director Maxwell as soon as I know if they're going to be able to come so you are prepared."

He laughed, "Don't really need any preparation, Colleen, now I take each moment as I come to it, with God's help."

"I know what you mean."

Favored

*

The sleek vehicle pulled into the lot of THE 95 before six o'clock that evening. They piled out and entered the restaurant. The place was packed, and Colleen ran to the back to hug Cletus and Jolene. "I'm home. Do you need help? I feel well rested and could work a few hours if you need me."

Cletus pushed her away with a grin… "Could always use your help. Better get washed up and slip on an apron and take the order of our Sheriff and his lady." He was dishing up a bowl of chili… "Say, ain't you hungry too?"

"Nah. I'll wait and take a snack home when I get off. I'd rather wait." She laughed as she headed to the break room.

Boyd and Amanda seated themselves at the bar and ordered tea. He asked, "How're you taking the turn this case has taken?"

"To tell the truth, I'm not at all surprised. I had a deep premonition about this outcome. What with the new baby on the way… Eddie spending every off minute with her, and knowing he's well taken care of and content with his life. And when she saw how contrite Junior was, I never for a moment thought she'd need to charge him. In fact… want to hear what I think about their situation?"

"Sure. You got some crystal ball?"

"Sort of." She took a bite of the big burger and spoke gently holding her lips together. "I think those two will ultimately get together… probably get married."

"Nah… it'll never happen. She's been too hurt to ever consider that."

"Just wait until that baby's born. A constant reminder of who it's daddy is will pull stronger than past memories. Besides, Colleen said she wouldn't allow anything of the trauma of the attack to define her future with the baby."

"Wonder what it is?"

"I hope it's a girl. She'll be Eddie's little sister."

"Eddie'll need a little brother to teach all about hunting and fishing."

They laughed and continued enjoying the food.

"You going to see if you can locate Maizie?"

"Um huh. I'll see what I can do tomorrow. I think I can find her easy enough.

"Can we ride down for the graduation together?"

"Sure. I'll see if Colleen convinces Bobby and Ashe to go… if they do, she'll probably ride with them and Eddie."

"His graduation from Hope House will pinpoint the place of a new beginning."

"Yeah, kind of… his real new beginning began the day he broke open and saw the wasted past of his life up 'til then." Holding still, Boyd looked upward and sighed. "They said the day Max baptized him it was cloudy… overcast, and the moment he brought him up out of the water that the clouds broke, and a raft of sunshine came down and lit up that lake." He shrugged. "Makes chills run up and down my arms to think about it."

"I can understand that. His change has been truly miraculous… And speaking of miraculous… The fact that Colleen has decided to let Eddie stay with his daddy and Ashe, and not charge Bobby with kidnapping, as well as forgiving and not charging Junior with the rape and attempted murder is something well beyond miraculous."

"Yep… a couple of very favored men, I'd say."

*

Amanda took a break to the restroom while Boyd paid the tab. "We're heading out. Colleen, you want someone to see you home?"

"Thank you, Sheriff, but I'll be fine. Milford will see to my safety... I won't be here much longer, anyway. Thanks."

*

The following Sunday afternoon the dining hall at Hope House had the tables arranged in special fashion. There was a head table near the entrance with six chairs: Director Maxwell Peters in the middle, with two places to his right... Sheriff Custer and the Solicitor Amanda Harris. To the left of the Director were to be seated-in order of length of time spent at Hope House- would be Gordon Blum, then Cuthbert Woolsley, and last on the left would be William Travis Raeford Jr.

Down front were the honor tables hosting the families of the three graduates. There was a plethora of children running around with attendant adults needing to pay very little attention to them because the men still remaining at Hope House were taking them around the room and showing them the kitchen, the photographs along the wall of previous patrons and visitors... plying them with small treats of food before dinner.

As soon as Max saw the head server nod, he got everyone's attention and had them take their seats. As soon as the blessing was asked; the servers... all dressed in white uniforms began bringing filled plates to the guests. Teas, and waters were poured in the appropriate glasses, but desserts were held until after the dinner was finished. Maxwell did not believe in tempting the children or their parents with sweets until they had the opportunity to enjoy their meal first.

The tenor within the large hall was muted and contentment flowed. Everywhere anyone might want to look, they'd be greeted with nods and smiles. Boyd was thoughtful of the atmosphere, he could almost feel the love sweeping around the space. *This is the best place I could ever have sent Junior. Thank you, Father, for Hope House.*

*

By the time the Chapel Bell rang seven times, the sanctuary was already full. The graduates, all dressed in suits with white shirts and dark ties, were seated on the dais with Maxwell. The pulpit had been moved off to the right end, enabling the audience to clearly observe their graduates being honored.

After a few minutes, the din subsided, and Maxwell stepped forward to stand behind the pulpit. "Welcome." He bowed his head and said, "Our Father, you are welcome here above all. Bless us by your holy presence and place your Spiritual hand upon this gathering as well as ever upon these graduates. Amen."

He turned to look at the men. "Gordon, you came to this place nearly six months ago, but have comported yourself with great strength and have exemplified your willingness to listen, learn, and alter your previous way of life. We congratulate you. Now come and give this company your Testimony. Please."

The man-Gordon was tall, thin, and thirtyish… nearly bald. His suit fitted slack against his frame, but there was still a spring in his step and he stood front and center in front of the microphone. He cleared his throat and spoke. "Friends…

For the next ten minutes the audience heard the story of a life gone wrong from childhood. Many wondered how he'd made it through alive. The only person here for him at his graduation was his boss, a Mister Zastro Theopolis, who thought enough of Gordon to insist on him coming here. Literally saving the man's life.

Next up to the mike was Junior's closest friend-Cuthbert Woolsley. Cuthbert was a slightly built, knotty muscled, white-toothed man with a grin that split his black face like a shaft of sunlight in a coalmine. Junior loved him... as did his family. His wife, Sandra with their two children- Connie and Thomas (teenagers) sat proudly in the front row to cheer him on.

Cuthbert spoke into the mike long enough to have nearly everyone in the sanctuary weeping with the story of his fall... and then laughing with his exploits while here at Hope House. How Maxwell heard for the first time how Cuthbert had tried to strain up the bucket of milk the day ole' Bess had stepped her foot into the bucket before he could get it moved. As the laughter died down he knew he would miss this place... but not enough to keep him from his beloved and patient wife and children.

Last to walk to the center was Junior. He shifted on his feet a little and looked down at his family... a mother he'd not seen in over a year... his best friend-Bobby... his boss, Sheriff Boyd... and the love of his life ever since he could remember-Colleen. He began to speak, and the sanctuary sat in silence as they listened to the testimony of a boy that couldn't recall his first drink he was so young... back before high school. He spoke of how he'd found his best friend loved the taste of alcohol as much as he did... their dastardly deeds and dangerous escapades... how they'd both set their sights on the same girl and how he'd lost... trying to never let on how much it hurt to stand as best man at her wedding. How he'd commiserated with lies when Bobby would complain about his wife.

His expose' went on for quite a while until at last he began the recounting of the time he'd snapped and nearly killed the woman he loved with all his heart. He then spoke of his sojourn here at Hope House where God had finally slapped him down and lifted him up. He spoke of how his life was nothing like he'd ever even imagined it could be…

There wasn't a dry eye in the place. Even Maxwell had to get out his handkerchief. Colleen was weeping softly, but her spirit was soaring. Suddenly a thought came into her head: *I'll marry Junior if he'll have me. I know I've loved him too, and I'll never know why I chose Bobby. I hope it's not too late for us.*

After Junior sat back down, Maxwell rose and came to the center with three framed documents. He called the three men forward.

After saying a few words about each one, he handed them the framed documents. The congregation stood and applauded.

"Let us remain standing… He bowed his head and held up his hands and pronounced the benediction. After the 'amen', the crowd surged, and the families rushed forward to embrace their beloved men. Mister Theopolis grabbed his employee and happily said, "Come with me my son… we've a business to run. You know we open the doors at eight A. M. sharp and I cannot face the masses alone!"

Gordon, laughed… "I'm right beside you, Sir."

As the crowd began to thin, and most of the patrons of Hope House had left for other endeavors, Colleen and Eddie were in close conversation with Maxwell. Amanda was aware of them but had no idea as to the exchange between them.

Saying their goodbye's, Mazie and Junior were in tight hugs, with Mazie swearing she'd keep in closer touch now. Everyone was surprised that Boyd had been able to locate her since she'd found herself in Alaska with a James Birdwell-gold mine owner… 'The Blue Bird Gold Mine' was producing enough for him to provide Maizie with his own plane and pilot who flew her home and was housed at the Columbia airport waiting to take her back. Boyd knew right off that he didn't stand a chance in hell of bringing back any old feelings between them. Oh, well… In his heart, Amanda was quickly coming up from the rear, in fact he watched in his mind's eye as she swept past his old love, Maizie and crossed the finish line in first place… barely out of breath. He smiled and no one who saw it knew why. Boyd was content.

Departing the chapel proper, the only ones still gathered were Junior, Colleen, Bobby, Ashe, and young Eddie. Everyone, even Maxwell, had left. Junior and Colleen were in close conversation. "I'll walk with you up to the front. Boyd and Amanda are waiting for you to get your belongings together since they came prepared to take you back to Zacchary with them."

Junior reached out and took Colleen's hand in his. "Thank you for being exactly who I know you've been from the time I first laid eyes on you… the most wonderful and beautiful girl in this entire world. I hope I don't make you sick of hearing me tell you that I love you… I do, you know. I love you, Colleen. I love you. I will always love you. Give me the hope of a future with us together. Please."

She reached over in the gloaming light and kissed him. Bobby watched as did her son.

CHAPTER 35

Favored

Maxwell stood down front at the head of the wide aisle with Junior to his left. Standing next to Junior were Bobby and Eddie. To Maxwell's right, dressed in beautiful pale yellow chiffon dresses, stood Ashe and Jolene. The six waited down front with bated breath, to watch as Colleen came down the aisle dressed in a pink flowered gown carrying a small white Bible topped with a pink orchid and flowing ribbons holding everything together.

This was the first marriage ceremony for Maxwell and he was thrilled to be officiating at this very auspicious wedding of two very deserving people. He constantly prayed for God's blessings to rain down from heaven in a constant flow of joy.

The sermonette was spoken… the vows were taken… the rings were slipped on the appropriate fingers… and the pronouncement of "Junior, you may kiss your bride" brought hoots and laughter and they watched as Eddie ran to hug Junior and his mother and pushed between them as Junior laid a deep kiss upon his wife… at long last. He knew he was one of God's favored ones.

Colleen pulled Eddie to her and hugged him as she became aware of a strong movement of the child within her womb. *How favored I am, Lord. Thank you.*

Bobby hugged Ashe to him as they all exited the chapel behind Colleen, Eddie, and Junior. *How favored I am, Lord for the life you've given to me and my son. I thank you.*

Maxwell caught up to Junior and asked where Sheriff Boyd and the Solicitor were… why weren't they attending the wedding?

"Oh, they already had plans set for a trip to the Bahamas for their wedding down there. They said they wished we could all come with them… and were so sorry we couldn't."

The group laughed as they walked across the verdant lawns in the warm sunshine.

The End

And God said, "I will make all my goodness pass before thee, and I will proclaim the name of the Lord before thee; and will be gracious to whom I will be gracious, and will show mercy on whom I will show mercy."

Exodus 33:19

Cast of Characters

THE WOODARDS:

Colleen Rebecca Spires Woodard… aka Jane Dooley. Daughter of late Wilma Pirallo & Lester Henry Spires. Deceased brother: Lester Jr.

Albert Edwin Woodard (Eddie)… Nine-year-old son of Colleen.

Carrie… After school baby sitter

Robert Edwin Woodard… (Bobby) ex-husband of Colleen and father to Eddie.

Clifford Bagwell… Boss at lumber company Bobby worked at in W. Virginia. Son: Darren Bagwell.

Ashe Woodard… Bobby's wife of just over two years.

Brandy… Girl known by Ashe and Bobby

Adelaide Clark… Widow renting upstairs rooms to Bobby and Ashe. She speaks of niece Sylvia.

Tilda... House helper to Adelaide

Jefferson... House man to Adelaide – he has four sons.

LAW ASSOCIATES:

Boyd Custer... Sheriff of Zacchary, South Carolina. Divorced from Ruby Miller.

William Travis Raeford, Jr.... Deputy Sheriff. (Junior) son of Mozelle (Maizie) Hunnicutt & Wm. Travis Raeford.

Anthony Dickle... Deputy Sheriff. (Twisted Britches)

Nancy... Sheriff's clerk, secretary, and right-hand girl.

LeeRoy Hasgrove... Ex-military, hunter, sharpshooter, undercover spy for Boyd only. Son of the late Mae Hasgrove.

Horace Godbold & Frederick Schlick... Pair of SLED agents.

Talbert Lamar... Coroner

Amanda Harris... Solicitor. Divorced from son of Frank and Irene Harris. Children, Joey and Leslie. Ex-Joseph.

Murdock Murkowski & Sidney... Deputies in charge of the jail and inmates.

THE CREW AT THE 95 TRUCK STOP:

Milford... Owner of THE 95

Selma... Wife of Milford

Cletus... Head Cook

Jolene... Waitress

Margie... Waitress

UNDER CHARACTERS:

Chester Jones... Homeless WWII vet. (nicknamed Colonel)

David Abner... Preacher in Zacchary. Wife, Mary

David Zimmerman... Country Club owner.

Doctor Hatfield... Works at Zacchary Hospital.

Blanch... Nurse in Zacchary.

Doctor Nelson Bradley... Director of Lucy Barnard Women's Clinic.

Betty Copeland... Nurse in Lucy Barnard Women's Clinic.

Christine... Nurse in Lucy Barnard Women's Clinic.

Rev. Dawson... Chaplain in Lucy Barnard Women's Clinic.

Otis Barnard... Adopted son of late Lucy Barnard

Richard Barnard... Son of late Lucy Barnard

Willie Wilcox... Newspaper Editor.

Jerry Arnold... Reporter.

Bess Arnold... Photographer.

Todd Willingham... Funeral Home owner.

Fowlard Brothers... Grave diggers.

Sarah Craig... Postal Carrier. Married to Melvin.

Graham Trublood... Owner of Lumber Company in Zacchary

Paulie... Pawn Shop owner in Zacchary

Slade Mellencamp... Shady character in Zacchary

Ansel Triplin... Mellencamp's lawyer from Atlanta

Lulu Watts... Town gossip

Doctor Tillage... Works with AA in Orangeburg

Clara & Justine Wilson... Cleaning Women

Spearman... Farmer from the past

James Birdwell... Owner of the Blue Bird Gold Mine in Alaska

HOPE HOUSE:

Maxwell Peters... Owner, Director, Pastor, Mentor

Cuthbert Woolsley... Man at Hope House

Sandra Woolsley... Wife of Cuthbert, and Connie and Thomas-teenaged children

Gordon Blum... Man at Hope House

Zastro Theopolis... Gordon's Boss

Taylor Simpson, Archibald Lamar, Gordon, and Richard... Men at Hope House

Clarence Bishop... Dispensary Doctor

Doctor Christian Taylor... Psychiatrist

Michael Angelo... Assistant to Doctor Taylor

About the Author

Priscilla was born in the mill village in Whitmire, South Carolina during the height of the 'great depression'. She displayed-from a very early age, the propensity toward art, but her father, being a strict disciplinarian stifled any creativity. Never encouraged and protected by her mother from her father's decidedly anti-artistic bent, Priscilla was further stifled. She found an outlet and some sense of fulfilment through her days of freedom at school. Excelling in her school studies; she found English and Literature to be especially rewarding and soon discovered a penchant for writing.

After graduating from high school, she moved away from her parents and her oppressive existence. Several months later she met and ultimately married handsome Clemson ROTC Cadet, William A. Shuler, Jr. Following his graduation, she embraced the life and worldwide travels of an Army Officer's wife. They raised four talented children who also benefitted from this unique cultural education. Following her husband's retirement after twenty-five years' service, and armored with a new enlightenment, Priscilla took stock and reignited her passion for art. Multi-talented, she enjoys oil painting, porcelain work, clothing design and construction, jewelry making, and writing.

Now at the tender age of eighty-six, she enjoys the freedom afforded by the written word. Her imagination soars as she contemplates new stories unfolding in the wings of her mind. FAVORED is her sixth full length novel.

Made in the USA
Columbia, SC
16 August 2022